ALL GIRL 3

LESBIAN EROTICA BUNDLE

VICTORIA RUSH

COPYRIGHT

For the uninhibited...

TURN UP THE HEAT IN YOUR LIFE!

To receive more free books and other steamy stuff, sign up for my newsletter.

Victoria Rush Erotica

VOLUME ONE

PEEP SHOW

1

After going over a week without any type of intimate contact, I was feeling especially horny today. In such circumstances, I'd normally go online to find an outlet to relieve my built-up sexual tension. But lately, I'd been finding that internet porn wasn't doing it for me. Sure, the girls were always hot and sexy and I could generally find something new and interesting to get me in the mood. But it all seemed so impersonal, so *manufactured*. Even my favorite lesbian webcam site had become a disappointment, with viewers swiping from one partner to the next, often right in the middle of a hot-and-heavy session.

I needed some real flesh and blood contact, or at least be able to *see* someone live. But I didn't just want to see and hear her, I wanted to smell her, feel her, *taste* her. Somebody who wouldn't exit the scene at the first sign of boredom, or as soon as she got her rocks off. I wanted to be with someone I could take my time with and enjoy the experience on my own terms. And *Tinder* was out of the question, since I didn't have the time or the energy to vet the candidates, nor string along the ones whose profile never seemed to align with their real personas.

After trolling through the usual online sources, I decided to try something new. I clicked on the latest issue of the Windy City Times, Chicago's long-time LGBTQ newspaper. At least here, I knew I'd be able to find authentic lesbian, bi, and trans girls. Among the litany of gay bar postings, I found an unusual listing in the classified section. Under the headline *Nude Casting Call* was an ad for open auditions at the local theater company. Intrigued, I clicked on the Details tab and began to read the full description:

> *The Bijou Theater is looking for uninhibited people who are interested in staging solo performances in the nude. With a king-size bed as your primary prop, your goal is to arouse and titillate a live audience using only your body and your wild imagination. There will be boys-only, girls-only, and mixed couples events, so you can cater your performance to your own sexual preference or mix it up as you see fit.*
>
> *A winner will be chosen after each audition based on audience response, with the winners moving on to regional semi-finals and finals. The Grand Prize winner will win an all-expense-paid vacation for two to the Desire Riviera Maya Resort in Puerto Morales, Mexico. Exhibitionists and voyeurs alike are encouraged to attend. Come one, come all!*

Holy shit, I thought, suddenly aware of the growing dampness in my panties. The idea of watching someone perform an erotic routine for a live audience definitely got my motor running. This wasn't some sleazy dive bar or strip club where the girls performed nude dances in front of a bunch of leering men. This was a legitimate theater where amateur performers volunteered to display their naked bodies to a group of of anonymous strangers in a darkened auditorium. And I could *choose* the target audience–no sweaty old men, no creepy lap dances, no private rooms where the girls were paid for private favors. I could just sit back and enjoy the show in the privacy of my own darkened alcove.

But what exactly did they mean by *solo performances*? Just how far did these performances go? Did they touch their bodies only superficially, simulating sex acts like a typical stripper? Or did they caress themselves in their most private regions, with the purpose of genuinely getting themselves and their onlookers off? The presence of a bed on the stage suggested it would be more than just a typical erotic dance. And how much audience participation would there be in the production? Were spectators allowed to actively stimulate *themselves* in the dark while they watched the performers on stage?

The more I thought about it, the more turned on I got imagining how exciting it would be to take in a live performance. Hell, if the conditions were right and the security was good enough, I might be tempted to give it a go myself. But first, I needed to check it out from the protection of the viewing gallery. At least there I'd be able to get my rocks off watching somebody else in the relative safety of a darkened auditorium. We could *both* take our time to ramp up our desire, knowing the only consideration was maximizing everyone's viewing pleasure and satisfaction.

I clicked on the Calendar tab and noticed a selection of dates highlighted in different colors and markings. Pink shading signified ladies-only nights, blue was men-only, and green was open to both sexes. A downward-sloping diagonal line through the box meant the show was sold out for new audience members, and an upward-sloping line meant auditions had been fully booked for that day's event. Scrolling through the pink-shaded boxes, I saw that the next three week's events were X'd out, indicating there was no room for either performers or attendees. The next available ladies night only had one line crossed through it, so I click on the date and booked a ticket immediately.

As I leaned back in my chair, imagining myself watching a pretty girl caressing herself on stage, I pulled down my panties and began rubbing my inflamed clit.

This is going to be interesting, I thought.

When the audition night finally arrived, I went to the theater and presented my online ticket to the attendant. A few other girls were waiting along with me behind the turnstiles, and after security checked our driver's licenses to verify our age and sex, they handed each of us a small bag and we entered the darkened theater, locating the closest seats to the stage. I peered in the bag and saw that it contained two items: a disposable plastic seat cover and a small box of Kleenex tissues. I smiled knowingly, then carefully spread the latex cover over the top of my chair. When I sat down and peered around me, I noticed that the room was only half full. Most of the seats were occupied by lone viewers with at least two or three open spaces separating them. I nodded, happy with the way the theater had set everything up for the maximum privacy and comfort of the spectators.

But I noticed there was also a sprinkling of same-sex couples strewn about the theater who were giggling and making out in their private cubbyholes. There was just enough light to notice that everybody was female, but not enough to establish their identities. Suddenly, the lights dimmed and a middle-aged woman walked out onto the middle of the stage under a bright spotlight. I recognized a familiar shape in the shadows behind her, and my heart began to flutter knowing that a nude performer would soon be lying on the bed, giving us a show to remember.

"Good evening, *ladies and voyeurs!*" she announced, holding the mic to her mouth. "Are you ready for some uniquely stimulating entertainment?"

A few people whooped and hollered, while others clapped excitedly. I wondered how many in the audience were 'regulars' who were there mostly to pass judgement on the performances, versus the first-timers like me who were there mostly for the intrigue and the stimulation.

"Those of you who've been here before already know the rules," the woman continued. "But allow me to educate the rest of the crowd to ensure the safety and satisfaction of all participants."

The buzz in the theater suddenly subsided as everyone allowed the MC to finish her briefing.

"Audience members are permitted to encourage the performers with verbal feedback, but we ask that you keep it upbeat at all times. Many of our performers are first-time auditioners, and we wish to provide them with a positive environment to express themselves openly. At the end of each performance we'll ask for your collective feedback to help us judge who should be moved on to the next stage of the competition. No booing or cat-calls–only clapping or cheering to reflect the degree to which you felt entertained. As always, we ask you to remain in your seats until the end of each performance unless you need to use the restrooms in the rear of the theater. For the safety and privacy of every performer, no one will be permitted to approach the stage at any time. Anyone breaking these rules will be promptly escorted out of the theater."

The woman paused for a moment to make sure everyone understood the ground rules. I nodded my head, beginning to appreciate the level of safety and security afforded the performers and audience members alike.

"Any questions?" the MC asked.

The room filled with silence, as everybody anticipated the next move.

"All right then," she said, swinging her arm to the side of the stage where the spotlight focused on a closed curtain hanging in the wings. "Let the show begin!"

As she receded to the opposite side of the stage, the curtain parted and a young woman looking to be in her late teens or early twenties tiptoed out onto the stage wearing a thin bathrobe. She glanced shyly toward the darkened auditorium, then walked purposefully across the stage to the king-size bed, now brightly illuminated under two criss-crossing spotlights. When she reached the edge of the bed, she paused for a moment then pulled her robe off her body and hung it on the side of the headboard, quickly slipping under the linen sheets.

I was able to catch just enough of her naked body to see that she had a petite frame and an agile figure. Her ass was firm and round, and her legs tapered with the grace of a short-track sprinter. I wondered if she might have been a college athlete. Because she'd turned her body away from the audience as she got under the covers, I wasn't able to see much of her upper body, which she'd kept carefully covered with crossed arms. But her face was young and pretty, with the plump skin, full eyebrows, and the unruffled hairstyle of a carefree adolescent.

My pussy twitched as I watched her climb into the bed, pulling the sheets high up under her neck with two hands. I smiled at how shy she was and wondered what had prompted her to participate in such an event if she felt so nervous about displaying her body. Maybe it had been a dare between her and her friends, or maybe her boy or girlfriend had put her up to it, or maybe she just wanted to experience the excitement of being naked in a room full of strangers. Either way, I found the whole premise highly stimulating, and I squirmed in my seat as I found myself getting more turned on by the moment.

I'd decided to wear a mid-length skirt and button-up blouse with no underwear underneath to provide maximum freedom of movement in the event I had the opportunity to touch myself. As I watched the girl lower one hand down the front of her abdomen under the thin sheet, my legs began to spread apart unconsciously. She still held the covers tightly under her chin with one hand, but the flimsy fabric meandering like a snake left little doubt what she was doing. At first, she teasingly cupped one of her breasts with her free hand, pinching the nipple with her fingers as her eyes darted tentatively around the darkened theater. I could tell she was nervous and excited at the same time, and I was happy she couldn't see any of our faces to embolden her actions.

Mmm, a few people in the audience hummed, encouraging her to continue. The girl smiled then inched her hand lower down her abdomen. When it reached the top of her hips, I saw her fingers probe the area near the base of her mound, and her face twitched when she found her sensitive spot. As she began to circle her fingers over her love button, my own fingers began to inch under my skirt toward my tingling gland. There was something incredibly sexy about watching a young girl touch herself under the covers, knowing that everyone's eyes in the room were glued on her.

With the murmurs from the audience turning from hums of approval to gentle moans, the girl slowly began to spread her legs, as the movement of her hand between her legs started to speed up. I could see her chest beginning to rise and fall as her desire began to mount, and she tried to keep a straight face as her lips puckered and her eyelashes batted intermittently while a gentle flush began to spread over her cheeks.

"Show us more!" one of the couples in the corner yelled.

The girl stopped moving for a moment, temporarily taken aback by the intrusion, then she slowly lowered the cover down to the base of her hips. Her tits were small but perky, resting high on her chest in a sexy crescent shape, with large areolas and dark nubs. She lifted her other hand from under the sheet and cupped both of them, pinching her hardening nipples between her fingers.

"*Yes,*" somebody purred a few rows in front of me.

Emboldened by the audience's reaction, the girl soon traced one hand back down under the sheets and resumed stimulating her pussy. As I watched the sheets tenting and puffing from the action of her hand, I slipped my own hand under my skirt and began mimicking her movement, stroking and caressing my little man-in-the-boat. I didn't know exactly why, but I found the experience of watching a live girl touching herself in a darkened theater much more arousing than watching somebody masturbate online.

I was dying to see more of her body and just when I was about to encourage her to pull the sheets down a little further, someone else in the audience beat me to it.

"Let us see your pretty pussy," someone called from the back of the theater.

The girl paused for a moment, unsure how much she wanted to reveal. Then she drew her legs back together and pulled the covers down over her knees. I could see her hairy muff sitting on top of her mound, glistening from the juices she'd been spreading over the area with her free hand. She began to separate her legs, then suddenly stopped, not ready to reveal her most private areas to a room full of strangers. But her heaving chest indicated that she was still turned on and desperate to touch herself.

Suddenly, she flipped over onto her stomach, placing both of her hands under her crotch with her legs tightly closed. As I watched her buttocks flexing and her hips pressing rhythmically down onto the mattress, it became apparent to everyone watching exactly what she was doing with her hands. While her hips began to flop up and down on the mattress, her mouth spread open as a flush rolled over her face.

Fuck, I murmured to myself, watching her jill herself under her stomach. *That is so hot!*

Seeing her masturbating so demurely with her pretty ass and back toward us was somehow even more of a turn-on than watching her close-up. I thrust my fingers inside my cunt and began fucking myself more vigorously, imagining myself straddling her with a strap-on dildo.

God, how I'd like a piece of that pretty ass.

"Spread your legs further apart!" someone called from the other side of the theater.

As if on cue, the girl began to spread her thighs until they were separated about thirty degrees apart. I could now see her fingers moving rapidly between her cleft with the underside of her glistening slit poking tantalizingly between her pink globes.

As the sound of impassioned sighs and moans began to spread around the theater, I glanced around me and noticed the telltale sign of movement in the adjacent seats. Many of the girls in my row had their legs spread wide apart as they stroked their pussies while they watched the pretty girl on the stage grow increasingly excited. I glanced at one of the couples in the corner and saw that one girl had her leg raised over the armrest while her partner rammed her fingers into her snatch as she kissed her passionately.

Suddenly, the girl on the stage began to moan more loudly as she angled her ass upwards, spreading her knees further apart. We could now see her entire glistening vulva, highlighted by the twin spotlights shining on her ass, from her pretty pink pucker down past her slit all the way to her hairy muff. As she sped up the movement of her right hand circling her clit, she reached further down between her legs with her other hand and inserted two fingers inside her hole.

She was now unashamedly fucking herself with two hands for the entire theater to see, with no further impediments, or hint of shyness. I could hear the sound of other fingers sloshing in and out of pussies all around me as other horny audience members rammed themselves in sympathy with the girl on the stage. Within seconds, a crimson flush spread over the girl's cheeks and her buttocks began to tremble. As her knees began to wobble from side to side, she squealed like an injured animal, caught up in the throes of a powerful orgasm.

Watching her come in full view of the surrounding audience was more than I could bear, and I arched my back, clamping down hard over my fingers, spraying my pent-up juices all over the metal back of the seat in front of me. As soft gasps and groans emanated from every corner of the theater, the turned-on crowd released their own pent-up pleasure in tandem with the pretty co-ed. I glanced over at the lesbian couple in the corner and saw the girl with her leg over the armrest convulsing in pleasure as her partner rammed her fist into her while they both watched the stage, transfixed by the erotic performance.

When the pretty coed finally stopped shaking, she pulled the sheets back up over her body and the stage darkened, as the spotlight shifted to the curtains on the opposite side of the rostrum. The MC walked back out onto the platform, holding a small device in her hand.

"What did you guys think?" she asked, pointing her smartphone out to the crowd. "Was that worthy of an encore appearance?"

"Woo-hoo!" some audience members hollered.

I noticed a needle swing clockwise on the decibel-reading app.

"Let's give the young lady a *proper* round of applause," the MC hollered. "Show her how much you all *really* enjoyed the performance!"

The crowd erupted in applause and cheering, demonstrating their appreciation and satisfaction with the performance. I noticed the needle swing about sixty percent of the way around the circle, and the MC turned the device around to register the results.

"Let's take a little breather while we give our next performer a few minutes to prepare," she nodded. "But compose yourselves, because the next performer is a crowd favorite!"

As the woman strolled back into the shadows, a group of stage-hands began remaking the now empty bed with a fresh set of linens.

I wish they'd offer us a similar turndown service, I thought as I wiped the back of the seat in front of me with one of the napkins provided in my care package. *Because if that girl only justifies a rating of sixty percent, I'm going to need some fresh towels before this evening is over.*

<h1 style="text-align:center">2</h1>

s I watched the next three performers, I grew increasing
aroused by the sexually charged atmosphere in the room.
At the end of the evening, the prize for best performance
was awarded to an older, more seasoned actor, but I couldn't get the
image of the young coed shaking quietly on the bed out of my head.
There was something about her self-effacing nature that turned me
on like no one I'd seen in a long time. I went home that night and had
three more powerful orgasms imagining it was *me* planted between
her thighs instead of her hand.

But I had far from satisfied my thirst for this intoxicating production. I immediately booked the next available ladies-night audition
then spent the next two weeks practicing my own erotic act in front of
my full-length dressing mirror. I wasn't quite ready to go on stage and
bare my soul for a room full of strangers, but I found the idea incredibly stimulating, and every time I thought about it I came harder than
I had in a long time.

When the night of the next auditions rolled around, I was already
soaking wet by the time I entered the building's lobby. I looked
around me and saw a familiar collection of singles and couples
waiting to be admitted, but there was one pretty girl at the end of the

line who caught my eye. Wearing black tights and a loose-fitting, cropped t-shirt, her tight ass and plump breasts barely concealed by her open midriff got me even more excited. As I stole glances at her sexy body, dribbles of lubrication began streaming down the inside of my thighs under my pantyless skirt.

Everybody seemed too nervous to strike up a conversation while we waited to go inside, embarrassed by the obvious reason for our attendance at the event. Like a bunch of perverts in a peep-show theater, we just wanted to hide in the shadows while we silently got our rocks off watching the action on the stage. I turned my body sideways, trying to distract the girl's attention from the river cascading down my legs while pretending to fish around for something in my purse.

After presenting my ID to the security guard, I hurried through the turnstiles and walked into the darkened theater. It was more full than last time, but I found a secluded seat about fifteen rows back from the stage. As the lights began to dim in preparation for the main event, another viewer side-stepped her way into my row and stopped a few seats away from me. I looked up and noticed that it was the girl from the lobby.

"Is this spot taken?" she asked, pointing to the seat next to mine.

I glanced around the theater noticing a few other open spots slightly further back, but for some reason I didn't mind having my personal space encroached upon this time.

"Um, no," I said, motioning to the open seat. "Help yourself."

The girl opened her care package and spread the disposable seat cover over the chair then sat down, placing her purse on the opposite armrest. It felt a bit uncomfortable having someone sitting so close to me, but my rapidly beating heart belied my true feelings.

"It's a little busier than usual tonight," she said, spreading her legs apart to make herself more comfortable.

I glanced down between her thighs and noticed a dark patch in the crotch of her tight pants. Apparently more than one of us had gotten herself worked up in preparation for the night's festivities.

"Oh?" I said, pretending to be disinterested. "I wouldn't know–it's only my second time coming to this event."

"This must be my seventh or eighth time at least" she said, not letting me off the hook so easily. "When were you last here?"

"Two weeks ago, on the last ladies' night."

"I remember that one," she nodded. "That was the one with the cute college girl who needed a little extra encouragement to show her body."

"Yes."

"She was a hot little thing, wasn't she? But I thought she got cheated out the most erotic performance of the night. I guess the more skin they show and the more outrageous the performance, the higher the scores they receive from the hardcore regulars."

"Mmm," I nodded.

"Do you prefer girls?" she asked. "I mean to *watch*?"

"I guess so," I said. "I find them sexier, but I also feel safer around other women. I don't really want to be surrounded by a bunch of lecherous dudes jerking off a few feet away from me."

"I know what you mean," she said, lifting her sneakers off the floor, one at a time. "At least the theater keeps the place pretty clean. They probably have to send a hazmat team in here after each show."

I shuffled my ass on the latex seat beneath me and smiled.

"Thank heavens for these sanitary seat covers," I said. "I can't imagine sitting anywhere in this place without them."

"And the *napkins*," the girl said, waving one in front of her crotch. "You can never have enough of these things once the action gets hot and heavy."

I was about to introduce myself when the lights in the theater dimmed and the MC walked out onto the stage. But I hardly heard anything she said while I ogled the girl's body next to me. As she leaned back in her seat to get more comfortable, her cutoff shirt slid further up her abdomen, showing the bottom of her fleshy tits. The sensuous curve of her mounds taunted me in the shadows, and I squeezed my thighs together trying to quell my itchy clit.

When I looked back up toward the stage, a sexy blonde girl was kneeling on the bed facing the crowd with her thighs spread about two feet apart. She was wearing a full-length body suit with holes cut out over the tops of her breasts and crotch to reveal her private parts. The effect magnified the size of her breasts, highlighting her pink nipples poking sensuously out of the thin fabric. But it was the effect on her *lower* body than really got my juices flowing. The only part of her crotch that was showing was her bright pink vulva, shining like the petals of a flower surrounded by the darkened landscape of her tight-fitting leotard.

"*Fuck*, that's hot," the girl next to me hissed, spreading her legs wider apart.

The girl on the stage suddenly swung around with her back to the audience, straightening her legs to her sides as she slowly lowered her crotch to the surface of the bed, performing a perfect split. Then she tilted her ass slightly upward, revealing her pink slit shining like a conch shell on a barren beach. As I squirmed in my chair, mesmerized by the girl's erotic performance, my legs began to spread apart with a mind of their own.

"Do you mind if I make myself more comfortable?" the girl sitting next to me said, pulling her black tights down over her knees. "I'm feeling the need to give my pussy a little breathing room of its own."

"By all means," I said, now fully on board with the idea of having a partner I could enjoy the show with.

She pulled her tights down over her ankles, draping them over the back of the seat next to her, then placed her ankles on the seat rests in front of her, bending her knees as she tilted her hips forward. I could see her bald mound and protruding nub glistening in the reflected light from the stage as my own pussy began to dribble onto the seat cushion beneath me.

Some movement on the stage caught my attention, and I looked up to see the blond girl flip over like a breakdancer, slicing her legs open into a wide scissor shape. With one foot pointed tantalizingly toward the audience and the other nestled under her shoulder, she was practically *begging* us touch her glistening gash.

"*Damn*," my seatmate groaned, now unashamedly rubbing her

snatch with her right hand. "I'd sit on that pretty pussy and grind my cunt against hers *any* time."

I slid my hand under my skirt and began to circle my burning nub, thinking exactly the same thing. It had been a while since I'd felt another woman's wet pussy against my own, and I fantasized about kneeling between the blond girl's legs and lowering my hips onto hers.

"Mmm," I nodded as my body began to radiate in pleasure.

Hearing the sound of soft moans and sighs emanating from the amphitheater, the girl suddenly pulled her legs together and pointed them straight up in the air. The curl of her feet and the gentle musculature of her thighs as she flexed her legs reminded me of a ballerina, and I wondered if she might be a professional dancer. But it was the exposed folds of flesh between her tight buttocks that I was focused on at this particular moment. As they spilled out of her torn bodysuit like an open clam shell, my mouth watered imagining myself sucking her pretty pussy while she went through her poses.

Just when I thought it couldn't get any hotter, she lowered her legs into another perfect split framing her face as she peered out into the audience. She began to curl her body forward as she smiled at her hidden admirers while she rolled her fingers over her puffy petals.

"Fuck, yes," the girl next to me hissed, spreading her legs further apart until her knee touched my elbow resting beside her on my armrest. "That is one gorgeous pussy. I'd water that flower any day."

As my seatmate tilted her head back onto the backrest and sped up the motion of her hand between her pussy, the girl on the stage reached under the covers and lifted a strange-looking device into the air above her splayed body. It looked like a type of dildo, but not like anything I'd seen before. This one had deep diagonal grooves in the shaft, making it look like an oversize plastic screw. She tapped a button on the base of the unit it suddenly began to gyrate in a circular flapping motion. Then she held the tip against the opening of her pink slit and slowly sunk the rotating dildo into her hole.

While the crowd watched in mesmerized silence, she began to

shake her hips back and forth as she grasped her ankles with outstretched arms. The whole scene looked surreal–like she was some kind of bendable doll with an animatronic dildo flopping around in her snatch as she smiled out into the audience. But the flush spreading across her face quickly reminded me this was no act, as her mouth began to gape open from the pleasure that was spreading inside her body.

Suddenly the girl next to me turned to look for something in her purse and she pulled out a large dildo. I recognized the shape of it instantly, with its penis-shaped tip and protruding rabbit ears on the shaft. She tapped two buttons on the base, then plunged it deep inside her sopping pussy, ramming it in and out of her sloshing hole. Having one just like it at home, I knew exactly what was happening as she held it tightly against her with two hands. While circulating beads around the perimeter of the shaft stimulated the walls of her tunnel, the articulated tip rotated around in circles caressing her G-spot as the flapping external appendages straddled the shaft of her clit, providing intense external stimulation.

As I peered back and forth between the contortionist on the stage and the sexy girl ramming her pussy next to me, I plunged the fingers of my right hand into my hole and began groaning along with the rest of the audience. When the girl on the stage arched her back off the surface of the bed, bringing her face closer to the gyrating instrument flapping wildly inside her pussy, I could feel my own pleasure rising toward its inevitable denouement as my body began to tense up.

Suddenly, her buttocks and thighs began shaking as her head jerked forward and back in unison with the writhing serpent between her legs. I saw her sex flush spread up her long slender neck then all over her face as she grimaced in climactic pleasure.

"Oh my *God*," the girl next to me groaned as her own body began shaking in convulsive spasms with the pulsing vibrator buzzing between her legs. Seeing both girls coming so strongly soon put me over the edge as I slipped my knuckles past the opening to my pussy while I pounded my G-spot with my fist, grunting in a series of powerful contractions.

"Uhn, uhn, uhn," I groaned, feeling the pressure building inside my tunnel.

Just before I finished coming, I pulled my hand out of my hole, jetting my juices forward like a garden hose. The intense spray bounced off the back of the chair in front of me, sprinkling droplets all over the front of my seatmate's body. She looked up at me and mouthed the words *fuck me*, taken aback in surprise. I leaned over and kissed her passionately, cupping her quivering tits as she pressed the still-vibrating dildo hard against her vulva. When we both finally stopped coming, we flopped back against our seat rests, panting in exhaustion from the intense workout we'd both experienced watching the sexy scene on the stage.

3

"Holy shit!" the girl next to me sighed when she finally came down from her intense climax. "That was *insane.* I've never seen anything like that before, and I've been to a lot of these performances. Whatever that thing was that was gyrating in her pussy, I want one of those."

"I know what you mean," I said. "I've got a pretty extensive collection of sex toys at home, but I've never seen anything like that before. Watching her use it hands-free with her legs spread apart was incredibly erotic."

As the brightly illuminated bed and the sexy blonde girl receded into the shadows, the MC walked back onto the stage.

"Did you enjoy that performance?" she asked.

"Woo-hoo!" the audience roared in unison.

"Hold up a sec," the MC said, removing her decibel-monitoring app from of her pocket and tapping the screen.

"Now tell me what you *really* think!" she said, turning the device toward the crowd.

Everybody hollered at the top of their lungs, clapping enthusiastically. The needle swung ninety percent of the way around the arc before stopping near the end of the red zone.

"That's going to be pretty hard to beat," the girl sitting next to me smiled.

She turned and extended her hand over the armrest between us.

"My name's Ashley. I suppose we should introduce ourselves now that we've gotten to know each other a little better."

"Jade," I said, clasping her hand with my wet fingers. "Sorry about the mess–I guess I got a little carried away by that last performance."

"That makes two of us," Ashley said, removing some napkins from her gift bag and handing me a few tissues. "I think you need these more than I do," she said, wiping my juice off the front of her face. "I've never seen a girl squirt as much as you do. You should consider putting on a performance of your own. With your special powers, you'd have a shot at going all the way."

I nodded my head as I cleaned the back of the chair in front of me.

"It's crossed my mind a couple of times. I could sure use a free trip to the tropics. But I'm not sure I've got the nerve to take off all my clothes in front of a group of strangers. I'm enjoying things plenty enough from right here in the viewing gallery."

I watched Ashley remove the dripping dildo from her pussy and wipe it off with a napkin. "What about you? You put on a pretty erotic show yourself. With your hot body, I'm sure you'd get some very appreciative scores of your own."

"I've thought about it," she said. "I guess I just haven't found a strong enough reason to give it a try yet. I'm still thinking of ideas for what I could do that would be new and different."

After the stagehands finished remaking the bed, the MC returned to the stage to introduce the next act.

"That last performance received one of the highest scores in a long time," she said. "But if anyone can top her, I'm guessing this next act has one of the best shots. Prepare yourselves for *Sappho and Aphrodite!*"

The curtain at the side of the stage parted and two naked redheads emerged, walking hand-in-hand toward the bed in the center of the stage. They looked remarkably alike, with similar builds, height, and the same auburn ringlets falling gently over their shoulders. I wondered if they might be twins, and I turned toward Ashley, pinching my eyebrows in surprise.

"I didn't know they allowed tandem acts," I said.

"It happens every now and then," she nodded. "But most people prefer to go solo. It's hard to judge a tandem act in terms of who should move forward to the next round. Sometimes, the MC asks the crowd to rate each performer separately, but in this case these girls almost look like *clones* of one another. It would be impossible to differentiate the two when it comes time to evaluate their performance."

"Do you think they're *sisters*?" I said.

"I dunno, but if they are, that's just notched it up a couple of levels in my books. Let's see how far they take it."

As I ogled the figures of the two girls walking across the stage, my pussy twitched imagining them touching one another. Their skin shone like alabaster under the bright light of the overhead spotlight, their pink nipples glowing like beacons on the pale canvas of their bodies. Their tits were very small, making them almost look like adolescent boys with their flat chests and narrow hips. But when they reached the side of the bed and climbed onto the mattress, their curvy asses and sexy slits left little doubt as to their real sex.

"Mmm," Ashley purred, placing her feet on the armrests in front of her, spreading her thighs apart. "There's nothing like fresh girl meat to get me in the mood. *Two* helpings are making me twice as hungry."

My own pussy pulsed imagining them growing up together, playing in the privacy of their own rooms. Whether they were real sisters or it was just part of their act, I'd already bought into the theme as my juices began to trickle down under my ass.

"They're fucking hot, that's for sure," I nodded, hiking my skirt up to reveal my glistening mound.

"Damn girl," Ashley grunted. "You look pretty edible yourself. I might need to take you home once the show is over to have you for dessert."

"That can be arranged," I purred, giving her a playful wink.

When we turned our attention back to the stage, the girls were lying down beside each other, rubbing their bodies together as they kissed passionately on the bed.

"Something tells me this isn't the *first* time they've been together this way," Ashley mused.

"No," I nodded, my eyes glued on the stage. "I have a feeling they've had quite a few years to prepare for this moment."

As they intertwined their legs and began to grind their mounds together, Ashley and I began to circle our tingling clits with our right hands.

"Mmm," I moaned. "I'd love to feel their sweet bodies pressed up against mine right about now."

"Do you need a little *assist*?" Ashley said, raising an eyebrow and reaching over the armrest to slip her fingers under my blouse.

"*Fuck*, yes," I hissed, dying to feel someone else's hands on my body.

I spread my legs far apart and rested the underside of my knees over the adjacent armrests like the couple I'd seen at the previous show. Ashley took one look at my pink nub poking its head out of its sheath and placed her other palm over my pussy, caressing my folds with the tips of her fingers.

"Yes, baby," I groaned. "Play with my clit while I watch these cute girls. I want to imagine I'm right there in the thick of the action."

"You like flat-chested girls, do you?" she purred, lifting her fingers to circle my burning jewel.

"Yes," I panted. "I reminds me of my adolescent years."

"Mmm," Ashley mewed. "The great taboo. It's off limits now that we're grown up, but I remember experimenting when I was younger too. I bet those two have been playing with each other for a long time."

"Yes," I groaned, beginning to lose myself in the fantasy.

The two redheads suddenly separated and shifted into a scissor position, lying on their sides as they reached out and clasped hands.

"*Fuck me*," I groaned, watching the two girls rubbing their pussies together.

"Does that turn you on?" Ashley purred, slipping her fingers inside me as she trilled my clit with her thumb.

"You have *no* idea," I purred.

"Oh, I've got a pretty good idea judging by how wet you are," she said. "Are you going to squirt all over their pretty little tits?"

"Fuck yes," I groaned, getting more and more worked up watching the two girls tribbing their wet pussies together.

"What exactly would you do with them if you had the opportunity?" Ashley asked. "What did you use to do with your girlfriends during sleepovers?"

"I'd touch them in their private areas," I panted. "Kiss them, suck them, *probe* them."

Ashley peered at me with a sly smile.

"Trib them, mount them, grind your pussies together?"

"Yes," I groaned, reflecting back on my earliest sexual discoveries.

"Did you squirt back then too?" she asked.

"Not right away. Not until I went through puberty and began lubricating more heavily."

"Did you cum with your little friends?"

"Yes," I said, beginning to tremble from the imagery of the two girls scissoring on the stage, reminding me of my explorative youth.

"What else did you like to do with your pretty girlfriends?" Ashley said, using the show on the stage as a metaphor for reliving my childhood memories.

"Sometimes we'd play with toys..." I said.

As if on cue, one of the girls lifted a long green object from under the covers, placing it between their pussies.

A cucumber! I murmured, remembering the moment when my girlfriends and I discovered how much fun it was to probe our pussies with whatever phallic-shaped objects we could find. As the girls separated their bodies, placing the ends of the cucumber against each of their openings, my juices began pouring over Ashley's hands.

"Do you want me to place my little toy inside you while you channel fucking these girls?" Ashley said.

"Yes, please," I begged, desperate to feel my pussy filled up while I imagined fucking the cute redheads.

Ashley reached over and lifted her rabbit vibrator off her seat cushion and without even bothering to turn it on, she rammed it inside my pussy, beginning to fuck me with the dildo as she leaned over to kiss me. I turned my face toward her and moaned into her mouth as I peered at the spectacle on the stage out of the corner of my eyes. The two girls now had the double-sided dildo deeply embedded in each of their pussies as they ground their vulvas together, moaning in unison. I could see their arms beginning to tense up as they held each other tightly, while their passion slowly built toward a peak.

Ashley tapped the base of the rabbit dildo, activating the dual vibration functions, and I slid down in my seat, pressing the flapping rabbit ears against my pussy.

"Oh *God*, Ashley," I panted. "I'm going to cum baby. I'm going to cum so *hard*..."

As I watched the pre-orgasmic rash begin to spread over the chests of the two pale-skinned girls writhing together on the bed, my pleasure suddenly crested and I groaned a deep guttural growl. As the redheads began convulsing and wailing in union, the walls of my pussy clenched in powerful convulsions and I sprayed my juices out my plugged hole, ricocheting off the top of the vibrator towards Ashley's face.

While I thrashed in my seat squealing in ecstasy, she smiled at me, blinking her eyes between the sprays bouncing off her face while she held the vibrating dildo firmly against my vulva. Suddenly I became aware of similar noises in the theater as other viewers groaned in unison with the two girls shaking on the bed. The action of the two youthful-looking girls had brought back a flood of fond memories and it took a long time for me to stop coming as I watched them pleasure each other on the stage. When I finally came down from my high and collapsed back against my seat, Ashley looked over at me and smiled.

"We've *got* to get together soon," she mewed, lifting her dripping hand to my breast and pinching my erect nipple.

"Let's get out of here," I said, thrusting my tongue into her mouth. "I can't wait a moment longer."

"What about the rest of the show?" Ashley said, motioning to the MC walking back out onto the stage.

"*Fuck* the rest of the show," I said. "Let's make our *own* show. I need to feel your body next to mine before I go crazy."

Ashley paused for a moment, then peered at me with a sly grin. She raised herself out of her chair and sat her naked ass down over my still-fluttering pussy.

"Why wait any longer?" she said, tilting her pussy towards mine as she rested her arms on the seat rest in front of us. "Maybe we can have it *both* ways."

As she began to rock her hips against mine, I felt our clits merge as a new surge of energy rocketed through me. I grabbed her ass with both hands and pulled her closer toward me.

"Fuck yes," I purred. "Let's show these guys how it's really done..."

4

———

After the show, Ashley and I went back to my place and made love all night long. Both of us had ideas for what we'd like to do for our own auditions, and we experimented with different positions and pairings for many hours. By the time I fell asleep at three a.m., I dreamed of all the adventurous things we might try on stage. In the morning, I slipped on a robe and went downstairs to cook up some breakfast and Ashley followed soon after.

"Mmm–that smells good," Ashley said, smelling the bacon and eggs frying in the pan.

"I thought you might be hungry after our little workout last night," I winked.

"*Little*?" she said, raising her eyebrows. "Between the two of us, we must have burned enough calories to light a small city."

I handed her a steaming mug of coffee and sat down on the bar stool next to her.

"That was pretty wild, wasn't it?"

"Are you referring to the action on the stage or how quickly we landed in each other's laps?"

"Both," I smiled. "I don't think I've come so hard as when you were grinding your pussy against mine while we watched the show together in the darkness."

"Viewing a live sex act can be pretty damn stimulating ," Ashley nodded. "I think it's genius what they've created there. I didn't realize how much I enjoyed being a voyeur until I discovered this production. But I think I'm just about ready to flip things around."

"Oh?" I said, lifting the food out of the skillet and placing it on her plate. "You think you're daring enough to bare everything in front of a group of strangers?"

"They won't *all* be strangers," she smiled, caressing my arm with the back of her hand. "*You'll* be there, right? It'll be that much more of a turn-on knowing you'll be watching too."

She paused for a moment as she wolfed down another spoonful of scrambled eggs.

"But it'll be even *more* exciting if we do it together."

"You mean as a tandem act, or each of us separately?"

"Both. It will be exciting for us to perform solo, but we can step it up to the next level if we decide to get together. That way, at least *one* of us will have a chance to win the trip to Mexico."

"You're just hedging your bets in case I win it for myself," I said, crunching on a piece of bacon.

"Well, if we each perform solo, we double our chances. Will you be my plus-one if I win?"

"Or you can be *mine* when *I* win," I smiled.

"Then when we get together as a couple, we can wow the crowd all over again," Ashley said. "It can only *help*, right?"

"I think you might be onto something," I nodded, finishing the last of my breakfast. "But now I've worked up a whole different kind of appetite. Do you feel like going back upstairs and working on some of our routines?"

"I thought you'd never ask," Ashley said, sliding her last piece of bacon sensuously between her lips.

For the next couple of hours, Ashley and I bounced ideas back and forth as we play-acted our routines in front of one another, giving each other tips and encouragement for how we could ramp up the excitement level. Then we practiced every combination we could imagine for joining together while we watched ourselves in my dressing mirror. By the time we both fell asleep exhausted again, I felt I'd vastly improved my repertoire of girl-on-girl sex.

When the date for the next auditions rolled around, we tingled in excitement waiting in the wings for our turns to go on stage. The first performer was a pretty brunette dressed in a cowboy hat and pantless chaps. She carried a pommel-horse-shaped apparatus onto the stage, then placed it in the center of the bed and plugged it into the nearest power outlet. After screwing a diamond-shaped dildo into the middle of the saddle, she spent the next thirty minutes riding it like a bucking bronco, flailing her arms in the air as the plug vibrated inside her. By the time she'd finished riding it in the forward- and backward-cowgirl positions, Ashley and I estimated that she'd had least four orgasms.

The next performers were a tandem act, dressed in sexy super-hero costumes. The lower half of the Batgirl character's costume had been entirely cut away, with her naked ass and bare legs posing a sexy counterpoint to her well-camouflaged upper body covered with a black mask, tight rubber bodice, and flapping yellow cape. Her Catwoman sidekick had the front of her full-length bodysuit slit open down the front, pressing her large round breasts into a sexy cleavage exposed on the front of her chest. They'd had some additional props placed on the stage and the Catwoman character entered first, creeping furtively toward a nightstand at the side of the bed. She opened the drawer, peering nervously around her, then she tucked a jewelry box under her arm.

Suddenly, Batgirl entered from the other side of the stage and confronted the would-be burglar, placing her hands on her hips and shaking her head in disapproval. Catwoman pulled out a whip and snapped it toward her adversary, but the Batgirl used her quick reflexes to sidestep the rippling cord. Then she pulled a foam boomerang out of her utility belt and flung it at Catwoman, striking her in the head as she fell to the floor, pretending to be unconscious. She then carried the girl to the bed and tied her to the four bedposts using wrist ties from her utility belt, spreading her arms and legs in a wide V-shape.

It was only then that I noticed the crotch of Catwoman's tights had also been split open, revealing her pink vulva surrounded by the black bodysuit. As she woke up from her stupor and took stock of her predicament, she sneered at Batgirl, flailing her body helplessly against her binds. Batgirl simply smiled back at her and reached into her utility belt, pulling out a large penis-shaped vibrator. She flipped a button on the base and the dildo began buzzing and throbbing loudly. As Batgirl lowered it toward her captive's open crotch in a threatening gesture, Catwoman thrashed her body on the bed, pretending to be frightened.

The whole scene was over-the-top campy, but somehow the appearance of the two skimpily clad superheroes pretending to battle created a highly arousing effect. Ashley and I looked at one another shaking our heads in dismay, wondering the same thing.

"I didn't know we were allowed to wear *costumes* and use *props*," she said. "Do you think our act is going to be interesting enough after this performance?"

"Let's see what else they've got in their bag of tricks," I said. "Remember it's not about the size of your package, it's how well you can use it."

As we peered back out onto the stage, Batgirl placed the vibrating tip of the dildo against Catwoman's mound and she suddenly stopped flailing as she lifted her hips to press the device firmer against her vulva. Batgirl peered at her devilishly, then pulled the vibrator away from her pussy as Catwoman feigned frustration. Then she held it against her flapping thighs for a few more seconds before yanking it away once again. They continued this cat-and-mouse routine for a few minutes until Catwoman shook her body angrily, looking at Batgirl with pleading eyes.

Batgirl picked the jewelry case up off the floor and pointed toward it with a disapproving stare, then motioned toward the nightstand where it belonged. Catwoman nodded her head in acquiescence, then Batgirl placed the container back in the table and held the vibrator high up in the air for the audience to see. They cheered her loudly, encouraging her to place it back on Catwoman's twitching vulva. But this time she inserted the huge phallus into Catwoman's pussy until it was fully embedded inside her. Then she proceeded to pump it in and out of her hole as Catwoman became increasingly aroused, moaning and writhing on the mattress until she climaxed in a powerful orgasm. When they finished their routine, the audience roared in approval, clapping enthusiastically.

"That's gonna be pretty hard to beat," Ashley said, knowing it was her turn to go on next. "Maybe I should have dressed up in a costume or brought some extra props."

"Don't worry about what other people are doing," I assured her, squeezing her hand gently. "With your hot bod and your sexy routine, you'll have them eating out of your hands in no time."

"Or hopefully my *crotch*," she smiled at me nervously.

"Exactly," I said. "Go do your thing. Remember, I'll be here watching the whole time getting turned-on along with you."

"Mmm," Ashley purred. "That'll help. Maybe I won't need as much lube after all."

I smiled back at her, nudging her out the curtain, and she walked toward the newly remade bed with her hands resting in the side pockets of her robe. We'd both agreed that her act would be sexier if she revealed her body in stages, teasing the audience about what she intended to do on stage. When she reached the bed, she climbed up onto the mattress and straddled the brass headboard, placing one knee on the pillow and her other foot on the opposite rail for support.

She began rocking her hips sexily on the top rail and opened the front of her robe, showing her plump tits sitting high on her chest. As she slowly slid her body toward the corner bedpost, she peered up at me and I nodded, circling my hand over my crotch to signal how much her act was turning me on. When she reached the end of the rail, she grasped the small brass globe topping the post and rolled her hands over it like she was giving it a sexy hand job. But she and I both knew she was actually lubing the ball with some tissues she'd hidden in her pockets. Then she lifted herself up and straddled the post between her thighs, lowering herself down a few inches.

To the audience watching from an oblique angle, they couldn't have known immediately what she was doing, with her robe still covering half of her body. But for me watching directly in front of her, I could see that she'd embedded the brass finial deep inside her pussy. When she reached back and pulled her robe off her body, an audible gasp rose from the audience when they finally realized what she was doing. With appreciate applause wafting up from the seats, Ashley placed both of her hands on the top rail and began to rock her body up and down over the brass bulb. As it became obvious she was fucking the bedpost, many observers began to moan while they stimulated themselves watching her erotic act.

When she peered back over towards me, I was squeezing my right breast tightly while my other hand fluttered between my legs. I nodded at her quietly as my body began to tremble in concert with hers, losing myself in her performance. Even though we'd talked about what we planned to do once we were on stage, I hadn't realized how sexy it would be to watch her first hand with the audience buzzing around us.

As Ashley became increasingly aroused listening to the reaction of the audience, she turned her body to face them directly, spreading her knees wide apart so they could clearly see her impaled over the bedpost. Her movements began to pick up in intensity and her neck muscles started to tighten as she approached climax. Suddenly she lurched forward, jerking her body forward and back from the convulsions racking her body.

As I watched her shaking in the throes of agony, I came unconsciously watching my new friend pleasure herself in front of the large audience. After many long seconds of quivering in pleasure, she slowly lifted herself off the glistening pole and pulled her robe back over her body, scampering off the stage in my direction. As the lights fell over the platform, the audience cheered loudly in appreciation of her sexy and original performance.

5

"What did you think?" Ashley said, scurrying up next to me.

"That was fucking hot," I said, holding her tightly as I motioned toward the still-buzzing amphitheater. "And judging by the audience reaction, *they* enjoyed it too. How did it feel being on stage? Were you nervous at all?"

"A little at first," she nodded. "But once I got that ball inside me, I wasn't thinking of much else. Other than watching *you,* of course. Knowing you were getting turned on watching me was more exciting than knowing everybody else was watching me."

"I'm glad," I said. "Did you enjoy yourself?"

"You have no idea," she smiled. "Let's just say the turnaround crew might need a little longer to clean up the bed in preparation for the next act.

"Speaking of which," she said, slipping her hand inside my robe to cup my quivering breast. "Are you ready to go out there? You seem a bit nervous yourself."

"That's just me still feeling excited from watching you. I've never felt more ready to do something like this in my whole life."

"Break a leg, babe," Ashley smiled. "Just make sure you don't break anything *else*." She held up her hands as I turned around for her to help me disrobe. "Are you sure you want to go out there completely naked?"

"It'll just get in the way," I said. "I just want it to be my naked body they're focused on. Hopefully that'll be enough."

"You don't need any props or extra embellishments," Ashley said. "You'll be doing something nobody's ever seen before."

"Wish me luck then," I said, hearing the MC come back out onto the stage to introduce the next act.

"You won't need it," Ashley said. "I'll see you soon."

I smiled back at her, knowing it would be sooner than anybody expected.

As the MC motioned toward the stagehands, the curtain swung open and I strutted across the stage, relishing every step as the audience took in my taut, hourglass figure. I'd worked hard to keep my thirty-something body in good shape and as I extended my legs with each step, wiggling my ass and holding my chest high, my body surged with fire. I was about to do something I'd never tried before, and the idea of touching myself in front of a room full of strangers electrified me.

When I reached the bed, I lay down on it face up and reached behind me to grasp the headrail with both hands. I could still feel traces of Ashley's lubrication on the bar, and it excited me as I pulled my legs up and over my head, showing the crowd my bald pussy and ass. A few girls hollered their approval, and I spread my legs into a wide 'V' so they could see my glistening bald pussy more easily. A few people applauded my limber body, but after the previous week's sexy contortionist act, I knew they were looking for something more.

I caressed the insides of my thighs, stopping tantalizingly short of my pink folds, then turned around and placed my hips against the headboard, tilting my head as I peered at the audience upside down. They cheered loudly at my taunting gesture, knowing it was just a warm-up for the main act. Then I lifted my legs straight up above my body and slowly lowered them backwards toward my head. I'd been working on my flexibility in the weeks leading up to the performance and didn't have any difficulty resting my toes on the surface of the bed a few feet behind my head.

At this point all the audience could see was the slit of my ass with my face concealed by my closed legs. As they continued to cheer me on, I began to spread my feet apart until my legs were separated about sixty degrees. I could have easily spread them further apart, but that wasn't the main purpose of my routine. I placed the palms of my hands over each of my buttock cheeks and pulled my hips further down, moving my dripping pussy closer to my face.

With my toes inching further down toward the foot of the bed, the audience slowly began to realize what I was trying to do. As a loud murmur spread across the auditorium, I watched my slit move ever-closer to my puckering lips. With my erect clit quivering only inches from my mouth, I tilted my head back and peered toward the audience again, licking my lips in anticipation.

Realizing I was only inches away from taking my glistening gland into my mouth, their cheers grew in increasingly loud as I pressed my feet further down the mattress, lowering my box closer to my waiting mouth. Even though I'd practiced this hundreds of times before, knowing that so many eyes were watching me from the darkened auditorium raised my excitement to a whole new level. As my juices poured out of my slit over the top of my mound, I pulled my hips forward with one last tug, enveloping my hot gland with my moist lips.

A loud gasp suddenly arose from the audience, who'd never expected me to accomplish this feat of gymnastic elasticity. As I began to circle my tongue around my bright red jewel, a series of loud moans emanated from every corner of the auditorium. The crowd's reaction to my unique form of self-stimulation only increased my excitement as I lowered my hips even further, stroking my glistening slit up and down with my outstretched tongue. It was obvious that no one in the audience had ever seen anyone do anything remotely like this before, and I smiled as I listened to their shocked reaction.

As I licked the sides of my labia, pausing for long moments to suck my erect clit, I spread my legs further apart so they could see my pink pucker shining between my ass cheeks. I was putting every part of me out there for display, and the eroticism of the act lifted my passion with every passing moment. As I began to feel my pleasure rising toward its inevitable peak, I turned my face toward Ashley watching from the wings, and I nodded my head gently.

We'd both choreographed this routine carefully, and it was *her* I really wanted to cum with, not just the audience. Ashley dropped her robe on the floor and began walking onto the stage in my direction. When the audience saw that I'd enlisted an accomplice into my sexy act, their cheer rose even louder.

When Ashley reached the edge of my bed, she positioned herself behind my hips, peering down into my splayed, glistening slit. She smiled sexily at me, then grabbed one of her tits and leaned forward, stroking it against my wet opening. As she slid it toward my quivering mound, I popped my clit out of my mouth and began sucking on her nipple, alternating between her erect nub and mine. As the groans from the appreciative audience grew louder and louder, we smiled at each other, knowing we'd created something new and memorable.

But we were far from finished titillating the crowd, and I was still aching to come. I'd been holding back my orgasm until she joined me on the bed and as she peered into my glassy eyes, she pulled her body back until her face nestled directly between my thighs. While I resumed sucking my burning glans, she slowly licked my slit downward until she reached my pink rosebud. Without pausing for a second, she began circling my pucker with her long outstretched tongue, as my face began to turn redder and redder in mounting ecstasy.

As I felt my orgasm begin to wash over me, we locked eyes and I grunted loudly as my pussy began to clench in powerful contractions. I squirted my pent-up juices out of my pussy all over Ashley's pretty face embedded between my quivering cheeks. With my lips locked over my twitching clit and my entire body convulsing on the bed, I watched the muscles on the underside of my vulva pulsing as I sprayed squirt after squirt over Ashley's face mere inches in front of me.

The theater was now awash in the sounds of simultaneous orgasms as girls jilled themselves excitedly watching the two of us joined together in one of the sexiest routines they'd ever witnessed. Ashley reached between her legs and moaned into my crevasse as she popped off with the rest of the crowd. By the time I'd finished spraying her face and my clit stopped pulsing in my mouth, she leaned forward and kissed me passionately between my legs. As we lay there together for a long moment reveling in the reaction of the crowd, we nodded toward each other knowing we'd created a once-in-a-lifetime performance.

But we still had one ace up our sleeves to guarantee that at least one of us would be moving forward in the competition. With a sly grin, Ashley raised herself off the bed and straddled her feet between my hips as she peered down at my dripping crotch. Then she slowly squatted her body down until her ass cheeks rested against mine. I pulled my legs forward a few inches and bent my knees, tilting my hips backwards her until our pussies touched.

As we began to rock our bodies together, I watched her labia twisting and stretching against mine while we moaned in delirious pleasure. I was already buzzing from my last orgasm, and as we angled our hips toward one another, our clits touched and we gasped when we felt our sensitive organs melding together. As her slippery ass slid effortlessly over mine from our combined juices still coating our bodies, she reached down to hold my hands. I intertwined my fingers with hers as I peered into her eyes, feeling another powerful orgasm beginning to overtake me.

The feeling of her erect clit rolling over mine as our asses rubbed together was sublime. Although we'd experimented with the routine in the days leading up to this week's performance, there was something about the audacity of performing it live in front of a crowd of strangers that raised the excitement level even higher for both of us. As Ashley's mouth began to spread open while she approached another powerful orgasm, she peered down at me and mouthed the words *I love you*. By now, neither of us were paying any attention to the moans and groans emanating from the audience as we gripped each other's hands tightly while our pleasure consumed us.

Suddenly, Ashley let out a howl as her body began convulsing overtop of my hips. Watching her come with her pussy joined together with mine quickly put me over the edge also as I began spraying out in every direction from the tight seal between us. While I watched the spectacle from my prone position with my juices splashing all over our tits and faces, I saw my rosebud clamping rhythmically inches from my face. When we both finally finished shaking in a uniform mash of merged flesh, Ashley dropped down onto the bed beside me and kissed me gently.

"If *that* doesn't get us a free trip to the Desire resort in Mexico," she panted, "I don't know what will."

I peered over toward her and smiled.

"Who needs a trip to Mexico when we've got all the stimulation we need right here?"

VOLUME TWO

MAID SERVICE

1

I t had been a long week on the road, and I was beginning to feel a bit antsy. I'd never really enjoyed business travel. The days were usually long, and my nights were often spent preparing for the following day's meetings. Granted, my clients took me out for a nice dinner afterwards, but those too were tiring, as I had to keep my game face on trying to land another hard-fought commission.

Being a freelance graphic designer was a tough gig, and I was always mindful of the need to coddle my buyer while not appearing to oversell my services. The idea of using these getaways for a quick hookup with a new acquaintance was out of the question. Not only was I usually too tired at the end of the day, but I had to keep a professional distance with my business associates.

I'd gotten up early to prepare for an important presentation later in the day, and after rubbing out a quick orgasm and having a shower, I sat down in front of my laptop at the small desk in my hotel room. But after reviewing a few slides of my PowerPoint deck, I paused and stared at the screen. This was the least fun part of my job, and I shifted the cursor over the address bar of my browser, preparing to type in the URL for my favorite lesbian website. I was still buzzing from my morning play time, and my panties were already wet thinking about watching some hot girls tribbing their pussies together. Just as I was about to take off my clothes and make myself more comfortable, I heard a gentle tap on my door.

"Housekeeping," a soft voice called.

Normally I'd ask the maid to return later in the day when I wasn't so busy. But I was caught unprepared and hastily pulled my jeans up before responding.

"Um–just a moment, please," I stammered.

I looked in the mirror at the front of the table and straightened my hair, trying to compose myself.

"Come in," I said, feeling my heartbeat returning to normal.

The maid opened the door and wedged her cart in the entrance, then hesitated when she saw me working at the table. She was younger and prettier than I expected, with dark brown eyes, soft caramel-colored skin, and puffy rosebud lips. I took a quick scan of her curvy figure and sat upright in my chair.

"Don't mind me," I said, feeling my pussy twitch unconsciously. "I'm just getting caught up on some work. Do you mind if I finish up while you clean the room?"

"Of course," she said. "I'll just be a few minutes."

She grabbed some fresh linens from her cart and disappeared into the bathroom. As I listened to her hanging up the towels and wiping down the counter, I suddenly remembered that I'd left my used vibrator next to the sink. Horrified, I glanced up and saw her pushing it to the side of the table while she peered up at me in the mirror. I blushed a deep shade of crimson and returned my gaze to my computer, pretending to tap away at the keyboard.

What the fuck, Jade, I muttered to myself, shaking my head in dismay. *Couldn't you have hidden the damn thing before you left the washroom?*

The maid seemed to take longer than usual to wipe down the surface as she rearranged my toiletries into a neat pile at the corner of the sink. I always felt a bit peeved whenever the housekeeping staff moved my personal effects, but today I was more put off than usual. Recognizing more movement out of the corner of my eye, I turned once again to see her leaning over and wiggling her ass as she finished wiping down the countertop.

She was wearing a one-piece black dress with a buttoned-up white collar and a short apron tied around her shapely hips. As she bent over and cleaned the vanity, I watched the muscles in the back of her legs flex while she swayed her hips in little circles. She caught my gaze once again in the bathroom mirror and smiled at me demurely.

Fuck me, I thought. *Are all the maids in this place this hot?*

I returned my attention to my computer and banged away at the keyboard as a jumble of random characters filled my slide. At this point, I had no idea what was appearing on my screen while I fantasied about kneeling between the girl's legs and slurping her pussy from behind. I could feel the wet spot beginning to grow in my panties, and I shifted uncomfortably on my chair, trying to distract attention from my aching clit.

When she emerged from the washroom, I turned toward her and noticed that she'd placed my purple Rabbit vibrator standing up on the side of the counter next to my toothbrush. The simulated penis head and protruding rabbit ears on the shaft stared out at me, mocking me for my absent-minded oversight.

Jesus Christ, I thought. *I wonder what she made of the unusual dildo. Had she even seen one of those things before?*

The thought of her touching my sex toy got me even more worked up as I imagined her pleasuring herself with the multi-functional device. Of course, I couldn't say anything, let alone acknowledge that she'd actually *touched* the object that had throbbed inside my pussy only a few minutes earlier.

As she strode toward my unmade bed, I was tempted to tell her to leave it as it was, since I knew it was hotel policy not to replace the linens until the next guest arrived. There wasn't really any need to make it up, since no one else would be seeing it for the remainder of the day and I'd just be climbing back into it in a matter of hours. But as I watched her glide around the side of the bed, I was so mesmerized watching her body in the mirror, I felt paralyzed.

As she leaned over the edge of the mattress, pulling the sheets toward the headboard, I saw her side profile for the first time. Even though her dress was buttoned all the way up the front of her chest, I could clearly see the outline of her breasts against the background of the stark white linens. Her tits were long and pointed, with wide separation between each peak, like she was wearing an old-fashioned corset underneath her tight uniform. With her light brown hair pulled back in a bun behind her head, I studied every curve and contour of her pretty face. Her cheekbones were high and round like a native American, but her cheeks were carved like a supermodel's. With her golden-brown skin and smoldering eyes, she looked like a cross between Jessica Alba and Jennifer Lopez.

Oh my God, I drooled, staring at her in my mirror. *How has this angel not already been swooped up by some handsome billionaire and whisked away to his private enclave? Was this her first week on the job and still too naive to know that with that body and those looks, she could write her own ticket?*

As she smoothed down the sheets and wrapped them around the base of the mattress, I leered at her tight ass, fantasizing about all the ways I'd like to fuck her. By now, my panties were so soaked, I'd formed a large wet patch in the crotch of my pants, and I squeezed my thighs together, trying to quiet my raging clit.

When the girl swept around the base of the bed directly behind me, I smelled her perfume, as a light breeze wafted over my shoulders. It smelled sweet and flowery, just like I imagined her to be. I couldn't make out the brand, but I resolved right then and there to go to the nearest department store at my earliest opportunity to find it for myself. Even if it didn't suit me personally, I longed to feel her scent on my body while I fantasied about rubbing our bodies together.

When she shifted over to the other side of the bed to repeat the sequence, I angled my head in the mirror to watch her ass in the reflection of the large picture window overlooking the street. As she leaned over, she swung one of her legs up to support herself while she propped up the pillows in the middle of my oversize bed, and I caught a glimpse of the back of her thighs and a small patch of white cloth between her legs.

Oh, I moaned out loud, imagining what she'd look like completely naked. I wanted this sexy vixen, and I wanted her *now*. But short of jumping on top of her and pinning her to my bed, I was completely at her mercy while I watched her go about her duties. Besides, the door was still ajar, and we'd have no privacy if either one of us had any amorous ideas.

She rearranged the room service menu and placed a fresh bottle of water at the side of the table next to me, then peered up at me in the mirror and smiled.

"Was there anything else you needed, Madam?" she asked.

I paused for a long moment as the words stuck in my throat.

I wanted to tell her how much I wanted to make a mess of her newly remade bed while I wrapped my legs around her and plunged my tongue down her throat, but I shook my head and sighed.

"No," I said. "Thank you for everything. I'm good to go."

She nodded at me, then pushed her housekeeping cart over the threshold, softly closing the door behind her.

Good to go? I thought to myself. *What a lightweight you are, Jade. If you had any guts, you'd have taken her in your arms and kissed her like a proper lady.* After all, she'd given me plenty of clues that she was just as interested in me as I was with her.

As soon as I heard her move her cart to the next room and knock on the adjacent door, I leapt to my feet and grabbed my Rabbit vibrator off the bathroom countertop. Then I tore off my clothes and kneeled on my bed, facing the desk mirror. As I plunged the phallus deep into my dripping pussy and turned the setting to max, I dreamed it was the pretty maid who was staring back at me.

I still have three days to get you into my bed, I murmured. *One way or the other, I'll have you before this week is over.*

2

———————

I t had been a long week on the road, and I was beginning to feel a bit antsy. I'd never really enjoyed business travel. The days were usually long, and my nights were often spent preparing for the following day's meetings. Granted, my clients took me out for a nice dinner afterwards, but those too were tiring, as I had to keep my game face on trying to land another hard-fought commission.

Being a freelance graphic designer was a tough gig, and I was always mindful of the need to coddle my buyer while not appearing to oversell my services. The idea of using these getaways for a quick hookup with a new acquaintance was out of the question. Not only was I usually too tired at the end of the day, but I had to keep a professional distance with my business associates.

I'd gotten up early to prepare for an important presentation later in the day, and after rubbing out a quick orgasm and having a shower, I sat down in front of my laptop at the small desk in my hotel room. But after reviewing a few slides of my PowerPoint deck, I paused and stared at the screen. This was the least fun part of my job, and I shifted the cursor over the address bar of my browser, preparing to type in the URL for my favorite lesbian website. I was still buzzing from my morning play time, and my panties were already wet thinking about watching some hot girls tribbing their pussies together. Just as I was about to take off my clothes and make myself more comfortable, I heard a gentle tap on my door.

"Housekeeping," a soft voice called.

Normally I'd ask the maid to return later in the day when I wasn't so busy. But I was caught unprepared and hastily pulled my jeans up before responding.

"Um—just a moment, please," I stammered.

I looked in the mirror at the front of the table and straightened my hair, trying to compose myself.

"Come in," I said, feeling my heartbeat returning to normal.

The maid opened the door and wedged her cart in the entrance, then hesitated when she saw me working at the table. She was younger and prettier than I expected, with dark brown eyes, soft caramel-colored skin, and puffy rosebud lips. I took a quick scan of her curvy figure and sat upright in my chair.

"Don't mind me," I said, feeling my pussy twitch unconsciously. "I'm just getting caught up on some work. Do you mind if I finish up while you clean the room?"

"Of course," she said. "I'll just be a few minutes."

She grabbed some fresh linens from her cart and disappeared into the bathroom. As I listened to her hanging up the towels and wiping down the counter, I suddenly remembered that I'd left my used vibrator next to the sink. Horrified, I glanced up and saw her pushing it to the side of the table while she peered up at me in the mirror. I blushed a deep shade of crimson and returned my gaze to my computer, pretending to tap away at the keyboard.

What the fuck, Jade, I muttered to myself, shaking my head in dismay. *Couldn't you have hidden the damn thing before you left the washroom?*

The maid seemed to take longer than usual to wipe down the surface as she rearranged my toiletries into a neat pile at the corner of the sink. I always felt a bit peeved whenever the housekeeping staff moved my personal effects, but today I was more put off than usual. Recognizing more movement out of the corner of my eye, I turned once again to see her leaning over and wiggling her ass as she finished wiping down the countertop.

She was wearing a one-piece black dress with a buttoned-up white collar and a short apron tied around her shapely hips. As she bent over and cleaned the vanity, I watched the muscles in the back of her legs flex while she swayed her hips in little circles. She caught my gaze once again in the bathroom mirror and smiled at me demurely.

Fuck me, I thought. *Are all the maids in this place this hot?*

I returned my attention to my computer and banged away at the keyboard as a jumble of random characters filled my slide. At this point, I had no idea what was appearing on my screen while I fantasied about kneeling between the girl's legs and slurping her pussy from behind. I could feel the wet spot beginning to grow in my panties, and I shifted uncomfortably on my chair, trying to distract attention from my aching clit.

When she emerged from the washroom, I turned toward her and noticed that she'd placed my purple Rabbit vibrator standing up on the side of the counter next to my toothbrush. The simulated penis head and protruding rabbit ears on the shaft stared out at me, mocking me for my absent-minded oversight.

Jesus Christ, I thought. *I wonder what she made of the unusual dildo. Had she even seen one of those things before?*

The thought of her touching my sex toy got me even more worked up as I imagined her pleasuring herself with the multi-functional device. Of course, I couldn't say anything, let alone acknowledge that she'd actually *touched* the object that had throbbed inside my pussy only a few minutes earlier.

As she strode toward my unmade bed, I was tempted to tell her to leave it as it was, since I knew it was hotel policy not to replace the linens until the next guest arrived. There wasn't really any need to make it up, since no one else would be seeing it for the remainder of the day and I'd just be climbing back into it in a matter of hours. But as I watched her glide around the side of the bed, I was so mesmerized watching her body in the mirror, I felt paralyzed.

As she leaned over the edge of the mattress, pulling the sheets toward the headboard, I saw her side profile for the first time. Even though her dress was buttoned all the way up the front of her chest, I could clearly see the outline of her breasts against the background of the stark white linens. Her tits were long and pointed, with wide separation between each peak, like she was wearing an old-fashioned corset underneath her tight uniform. With her light brown hair pulled back in a bun behind her head, I studied every curve and contour of her pretty face. Her cheekbones were high and round like a native American, but her cheeks were carved like a supermodel's. With her golden-brown skin and smoldering eyes, she looked like a cross between Jessica Alba and Jennifer Lopez.

Oh my God, I drooled, staring at her in my mirror. *How has this angel not already been swooped up by some handsome billionaire and whisked away to his private enclave? Was this her first week on the job and still too naive to know that with that body and those looks, she could write her own ticket?*

As she smoothed down the sheets and wrapped them around the base of the mattress, I leered at her tight ass, fantasizing about all the ways I'd like to fuck her. By now, my panties were so soaked, I'd formed a large wet patch in the crotch of my pants, and I squeezed my thighs together, trying to quiet my raging clit.

When the girl swept around the base of the bed directly behind me, I smelled her perfume, as a light breeze wafted over my shoulders. It smelled sweet and flowery, just like I imagined her to be. I couldn't make out the brand, but I resolved right then and there to go to the nearest department store at my earliest opportunity to find it for myself. Even if it didn't suit me personally, I longed to feel her scent on my body while I fantasied about rubbing our bodies together.

When she shifted over to the other side of the bed to repeat the sequence, I angled my head in the mirror to watch her ass in the reflection of the large picture window overlooking the street. As she leaned over, she swung one of her legs up to support herself while she propped up the pillows in the middle of my oversize bed, and I caught a glimpse of the back of her thighs and a small patch of white cloth between her legs.

Oh, I moaned out loud, imagining what she'd look like completely naked. I wanted this sexy vixen, and I wanted her *now*. But short of jumping on top of her and pinning her to my bed, I was completely at her mercy while I watched her go about her duties. Besides, the door was still ajar, and we'd have no privacy if either one of us had any amorous ideas.

She rearranged the room service menu and placed a fresh bottle of water at the side of the table next to me, then peered up at me in the mirror and smiled.

"Was there anything else you needed, Madam?" she asked.

I paused for a long moment as the words stuck in my throat.

I wanted to tell her how much I wanted to make a mess of her newly remade bed while I wrapped my legs around her and plunged my tongue down her throat, but I shook my head and sighed.

"No," I said. "Thank you for everything. I'm good to go."

She nodded at me, then pushed her housekeeping cart over the threshold, softly closing the door behind her.

Good to go? I thought to myself. *What a lightweight you are, Jade. If you had any guts, you'd have taken her in your arms and kissed her like a proper lady.* After all, she'd given me plenty of clues that she was just as interested in me as I was with her.

As soon as I heard her move her cart to the next room and knock on the adjacent door, I leapt to my feet and grabbed my Rabbit vibrator off the bathroom countertop. Then I tore off my clothes and kneeled on my bed, facing the desk mirror. As I plunged the phallus deep into my dripping pussy and turned the setting to max, I dreamed it was the pretty maid who was staring back at me.

I still have three days to get you into my bed, I murmured. *One way or the other, I'll have you before this week is over.*

3

———

I was so fixated fantasizing about the pretty maid for the rest of the morning, I was late for my scheduled meeting with my client. When I got to the office, I could barely concentrate on my presentation, flashing back and forth between her exquisite ass and her Gina Lollobrigida tits. Everybody else in my sphere of influence suddenly seemed so dull and boring. When my buyer invited me for dinner that evening, I reluctantly agreed, knowing I'd have an even harder time concentrating as I dreamt about slipping back under my covers, smelling her intoxicating scent.

When I returned to my hotel room, I lifted the pillow to my face and inhaled her heavenly aroma. For a moment, I contemplated rubbing out another quick one, but I only had a half hour to change my clothes and freshen up. As I leaned over the sink to reapply my mascara and straighten my lipstick, I glanced at my Rabbit vibrator still lying on the counter. Thinking back to how the maid had nonchalantly picked it up and placed it upright next to the sink made my pussy flutter in unconscious spasms.

Fuck it, I huffed, grabbing the dildo and pulling my panties down below my knees. I've still got a few minutes, and nobody will be any the wiser if I have a little fun before heading out to another boring client dinner.

Just as I was about to thrust the oscillating tip into my sopping tunnel, I heard another soft tap on my door.

"Turndown service," a familiar voice called.

Holy shit! I gushed. *Could it be the same girl? How could I be this lucky to see her again so soon?*

"Come in," I said, thrusting my vibrator into the side pocket of the hotel robe hanging on the back of the bathroom door.

When the girl opened the door and saw me in the bathroom, I peered back at her and smiled.

"I'm just getting ready to go out," I said. "Feel free to do your thing while I finish up."

"No worries," the maid said, leaving her cart outside the door and walking toward the center of my room.

I'd always wondered what maids did during turndown service, since I'd been away from my room or too busy to be bothered when they called. But this time, I was intrigued for a number of reasons, and after composing myself in the mirror, I walked out into the room pretending to collect my things.

"I always seem to be getting in your way," I said, watching her collect the throw cushions at my headboard and neatly arranging them on the bench at the base of the bed.

"Not at all," the girl said, laying my pillows down flat on the mattress.

As she worked quietly, I peered at her gorgeous ass, perfectly framed by the white apron tied around her waist.

"I always *wondered* what you guys did during turndown service," I said, looking for an excuse to keep watching her.

She turned her head and caught me staring at her skirt.

"It's mostly just getting the bed ready for you to turn into later this evening," she smiled. "And straightening up a few things like the breakfast menu and the minibar."

I smiled, imagining she was turning *me* over instead, while she ran her hands all over my body.

"I thought it might be something a little more exotic," I mused.

"Oh?" she said. "Was there something else you wanted?"

"Um..." I hesitated for a long moment. Then I chickened out and shook my head.

"No," I said, watching her fold the sheets down into a neat triangle at the side of the bed. "You're doing everything perfectly."

"Thank you," the girl nodded, peering up at me. "I'm still kind of new to this, so any suggestions are most welcome."

"I bet you find some rooms are a little more–*unkempt*–than others," I said, reflecting back on how she'd stumbled upon my vibrator resting on the bathroom counter earlier in the day.

"Some guests are a little neater than others, to be sure," she said, taking a little extra time to plump the pillows at the head of the bed.

"But yours is easier than most," she smiled, lowering her gaze to the cleavage showing in my partially unbuttoned silk blouse.

"Do people sometimes leave things behind?" I said, hoping to steer the conversation in a new direction.

"Oh yes," she said. "Everything you can imagine. Laptops, belts, pieces of clothing–"

"And *other* personal effects?" I smiled.

"Sometimes," she blushed. "But we store everything in the lost and found in case customers want to reclaim them."

"And if they don't?" I said. "Do the housekeeping staff get to keep them as the spoils of their work?"

She placed the breakfast menu on my side table with a fresh bottle of water.

"Not usually. The hotel tries to contact them, and if we don't hear back after a certain period of time, we usually throw it out."

"That must be frustrating," I said. "I once accidentally left an expensive coat in an overhead storage bin on an airplane and never had it returned."

"They couldn't find it?" the girl enquired.

"Apparently not," I said. "I always wondered if whoever cleans the plane simply didn't report it and kept it for themselves."

"That must have been infuriating," the maid said, heading toward the bathroom to check on my supplies.

"Not so much infuriating as embarrassing," I said. "It was the *personal* effects I left in my pocket that bothered me the most."

"Yes, I can imagine," she said, returning to the side of my bed carrying my robe and a pair of terrycloth slippers. "Was it something valuable?"

"Not in monetary terms," I said, widening my eyes as she laid the robe on the edge of the mattress and placed the slippers at the side of the bed. "Just little trinkets I carry with me to keep me amused on long flights."

She felt the lump in the pocket of my robe and reached in to extract my vibrator.

"Like *this* one?" she smiled, placing it upright on the night table beside the bed. "I don't think you'll want this falling into the wrong hands."

"It depends *whose* hands it is," I smiled at her with a raised eyebrow.

The girl paused for a long moment, as we ran our eyes over one another's bodies.

"Do you mind if I ask how it works?" she asked. "I've never seen anything quite like it before."

"*Oh my God*," I said. "You haven't seen the famous Sex in the City episode where Miranda introduces her newfound sex toy to her best friends?"

"No..."

"*Come*," I said excitedly. "Scooch down next to me while I show you what this amazing device can do."

I sat down on the edge of the bed and held out my hand, pulling her down next to me. Then I grabbed the dildo off the nightstand and tapped a button on the base of the unit. I handed the shaking device to the girl, and she wrapped her hand around the shaft.

"Okay..." she said, shaking her head. "That's not so different from most vibrators."

So she has used vibrators before, I said to myself.

"That's only one of *many* ways it can stimulate you," I smiled.

I tapped another button and suddenly the chrome beads embedded inside the translucent shaft began rotating in circles.

The girl's eyes widened as she felt the beads rubbing against her palm, and she took her hand away to inspect the whirring object.

"And get *this*," I said, pressing a knob at the base of the unit.

Suddenly, the head of the penis-shaped phallus began twisting from side-to-side like a possessed wobble-head doll.

"*Holy crap*," the girl said, shifting her weight unsteadily on the bed.

"You've never had your G-spot stimulated in quite the same way until you've tried this baby," I smirked.

"Is *this* the thing you left in your coat pocket on the airplane?" she gasped.

"No, I've got a smaller and quieter device I use to keep myself amused on airplanes. Maybe I'll show you that another day. But there's one *other* feature I wanted to show you on this special toy."

I tapped another button on the base of the unit and suddenly the silicone rabbit ears extending from the side of the shaft began fluttering rapidly.

"These little fingers stimulate your clitoris while all that other action is going on inside."

"No *way*," the girl said, holding her fingers over the flapping ears.

"Do you want to give it a try?" I smiled.

"Right *here*?!" she said. "What about the other guests–"

"It won't take long, *believe* me," I said, squeezing her thigh gently. "With this multi-talented toy, you'll be satisfied in a matter of seconds."

"I don't know..." the girl hesitated, peering toward the closed door. "I don't want to get into any trouble..."

"I won't tell if you don't," I said, thrilled that she was showing newfound interest in my toy. "Here–why don't *I* show you first?"

I pulled off my clothes and threw them on the adjacent bed, then kicked off my heels and sat back against the headboard, spreading my legs.

"Oh my God..." the girl panted, peering down at my glistening labia.

Maybe this business trip isn't going to be quite so boring after all, I smiled to myself.

4

"Watch and enjoy, sweetheart," I said, pointing the tip of the rotating dildo toward my opening. "*Mmm,*" I moaned as it sank deeper into my tunnel.

When I'd pressed the vibrator as far as I could into my hole, I tapped the button activating the throbbing head and pulled my knees up, rocking my hips in delight. The pretty girl sat frozen on the bed, staring between my legs while I rammed the artificial cock in and out of my slurping pussy.

"You like what you see?" I said, feeling my passion rapidly rising with her watching me only inches away. "Now for the coup de grâce."

I tapped the button to activate the rabbit ears, and the flaps began buzzing against my inflamed gland. I threw my head back against the headboard and pulled the dildo harder against my snatch.

"I'm going to cum, baby," I panted, feeling the wall of pleasure about to overtake me. "Tell me your name."

"Luna," she purred, shifting closer to me on the bed.

"I'm *cumming,* Luna," I groaned as she met my gaze, yawning her mouth open in sympathy with me.

She leaned in and sucked my erect nipples into her mouth, and I whined in ecstasy from the combination of sensations that were attacking my body.

"Fuck yes!" I squealed, as my whole body shook like I was having an epileptic seizure. "Suck my tits baby."

I couldn't believe this heavenly angel was actually touching me while I had one of the most powerful orgasms of my life. I hadn't come so hard and so fast in a long time, but there was something incredibly hot about this sweet girl watching me while I pleasured myself.

When I finally stopped shaking, I took the dildo out of my pussy and kissed Luna on the lips. She nibbled my upper lip and I thrust my tongue into her, pulling the back of her head toward me. She moaned in my mouth, and I reached out to grasp her pointy tits, squeezing them firmly.

"Now that we've gotten to know each other a little better, my name's Jade," I smiled, unbuttoning the top of her dress. "Let's get you out of these clothes."

"Okay," she said, peering toward the door uncertainly. "But I can't take too long. My supervisor will be wondering what's holding things up..."

"I won't keep you long," I said. "Maybe we can find some more quiet time later in the evening. Don't you want to give this a try before you go?" I lifted the vibrator off the bed and flipped my legs over the side of the mattress. "Just give me a sec to wash it off first–"

"No," Luna said, pulling the Rabbit out of my hands. "I'll enjoy it more this way. It's already lubed up and ready to go."

She stood up and untied her apron, then pulled her dress down over her hips and placed it neatly on the opposite bed. Then she reached behind her back and unclasped her bra, freeing her unusually shaped tits. She had large brown areolas and thick pointy nipples, giving her boobs in the appearance of butternut squash.

Very tasty butternut squash.

"Oh my God, Luna," I said, shifting over to give her room to sit on the mattress next to me. "Come here so I can suck on those melons. You have the most delicious breasts I've ever seen."

Luna sat down next to me, and I cupped her gourds in my palms, marveling at how buoyant they were given their pointy shape.

"Do you have any idea how beautiful you are?" I said, peering into her eyes.

"My mother tells me every day," she laughed.

"I meant with other *boys and girls* your age. Surely you must notice the way they look at you."

"I guess so," she said. "I always thought it was just because I'm slightly more *curvy* than the other girls."

"You're exceptional in *so* many other ways," I said, turning her chin toward me as I kissed her gently on the lips. "Have you ever been with another lover before?"

"Just some heavy petting with the boys at school. I've never been with another woman like this before..."

I pushed the Rabbit vibrator toward the side of the bed and pinched her nipples gently between my fingers.

"Let me show you what it's like to be touched by a woman. I think you'll find you don't always need *boy* parts to be satisfied."

"But what about the Rabbit toy?" she said, peering at my glistening vibrator lying on the bed.

"There'll be plenty of time for that another time. I'm staying at the hotel for a few more days. Now lie down while I worship your body."

I pulled the corner of the sheets toward the far end of the bed, and Luna lay down flat on the mattress. Then I pulled off her panties and lay next to her while we rubbed our bodies together softly. When she felt my breasts pressing up against her, she moaned softly and I kissed her, rolling my tongue around the inside of her mouth.

"Jade," she purred. "I love the feel of your body next to me. I've wanted you to touch me from the moment I saw you working at the desk."

"Oh *really*?" I said, pulling back in surprise. "You little tease. And here I thought you were ignoring me the whole time."

"How could I ignore you after smelling your scent on the vibrator you left on the counter? And I saw the way you were looking at me–"

"Were you bending over and shaking your ass more than usual to attract my attention?"

"Maybe..." she said, nuzzling her nose into the side of my cheek.

I smiled as I sucked on her puffy lips.

"Do you know what I've been fantasizing about all day long since I saw you?" I said.

"Showing me how to use your special vibrator?" she said.

"No," I purred. "Ever since I saw you leaning over the bathroom counter, I've been dreaming about licking your sweet pussy."

"I was thinking the same thing when I saw you staring at me."

"Did it make you *wet* when you thought about my face between your legs?"

"Mmm-hmm," Luna nodded.

"Spread your legs for me, baby. Let me feel what I've been dreaming about these last few hours."

Luna fanned her legs halfway apart, and I lifted myself up to position myself in her crevasse.

"God," I grunted, kissing my way up the inside of her thighs. "You smell exquisite. What *is* that perfume you're wearing, anyway?"

"Black Opium, by Yves Saint Laurent," she said.

"How perfect," I purred, peering at her dark labia framed by the thick patch of black hair resting on top of her pubis. "Let me smell your flower."

I pulled myself closer to her opening, then breathed in her perfume through my nostrils.

"You could attract any manner of pollinator with that heavenly scent," I said. "I feel lucky to be the first one to kiss you here."

"Yes," Luna panted, lifting her pelvis off the mattress. "Lick my pussy. Taste my nectar."

Normally, I would have teased her a little longer to build up her excitement, but I didn't need any further invitation. I lowered my head and enveloped her glistening jewel in my mouth, feeling her pubic hair brushing against my forehead. She tasted as sweet as honey, and I paused for a long moment, sucking her juices into my mouth. Luna groaned and pressed her mound harder against my face, and I extended my tongue, caressing the top of her lips.

"Yes, Jade," Luca purred. "Suck my rose. Spread me open like a blossoming flower."

"Mmm," I murmured, getting increasingly turned on by the botanic metaphor. I guessed there was a lot more to this intriguing maid than just a pretty face, and I was looking forward to learning about her other interests and passions. But right now, there was only one thing on my mind. Taking her cue, I lowered my head and pressed my tongue slowly into her cavity. Luna groaned and placed her hands behind my head, pulling me harder against her vulva.

"*Fuck yes,*" she grunted, gripping my hair between her fists. "Fuck my pussy with your tongue, Jade. I want to cum all over your face."

I was taken aback by her sudden raunchy turn, but her dirty language just got me more worked up as I felt my juices making a giant wet spot on the mattress between my legs. I grabbed the side of her thighs and pressed my tongue as deep into her as I could, then swirled it around in circles, tasting her syrup.

As she began to rock her hips against my face and grip my hair ever tighter, my roots started to sting, but I was so turned on by her mounting passion, I paid no attention. As she began to thrash her hips wildly against my face, I ground my own pelvis against the mattress, imagining I was fucking her with my cunny instead of my face.

Suddenly, she arched her hips off the mattress and wailed out loud as I watched her tits shaking like two melons in a hurricane. Her giant areolas stared back at me with their flaring nipples as I sucked her juices out of her twitching pussy. Luna held me tight against her vulva for many long seconds as her body twisted and convulsed against my dripping face. When she finally stopped cumming, she released her grip on my hair and flopped back against the pillows propped up against the headboard.

"Jesus, girl," I said, peering up between her legs. "You don't hold back, do you?"

"I guess I've been saving up imagining what this would feel like," she said. "Sorry if I got a little carried away. Did I hurt you?"

"Only in the best possible way," I smiled. "That might have been the sexiest thing I've ever experienced."

Luna turned her wrist to look at her watch.

"I've got to get back to work before I get into trouble. Will you have some more time for us to get back together between your business meetings?"

"Are you *kidding* me?" I said, feeling my juices dribbling down the inside of my thighs. "Screw my client. *You're* my new project for the rest of the week."

5

———

I arrived at my dinner appointment twenty minutes late, using the feeble excuse of a family emergency. But my buyer must have wondered just what kind of 'emergency' had put such severe knots in my hair and rumpled my clothing so thoroughly. But I hardly cared, reflecting back on the memory of Luna's hips quivering over my face. For the rest of the dinner, I barely heard a thing he said, as I nibbled on the red peppers in my stir-fry and swirled the red wine around my mouth, remembering her exquisite taste.

When I got back to my hotel room, I propped myself up against the bed's headboard and watched myself in the desk mirror while I fucked myself with my vibrator, imagining her looking back at me. I slept like a baby that night, then got up early to have a long shower in the morning. I wanted to be as fresh as possible when Luna returned later that morning to do my room. I kept myself busy fantasizing about all the things I wanted to do with her as I introduced her to the joys of lesbian lovemaking. But when the tap finally arrived on my door, it was a different-sounding tone that greeted me.

Hiding my vibrator under the pillow fold in the adjacent bedspread, I opened the door to see an older, frumpy-looking maid. I motioned her into my room, then collected my belongings in preparation for heading to the office. But as I watched her go about her duties, I couldn't help asking about Luna.

"What happened to the girl who cleaned my room yesterday?" I asked.

"We're assigned different rooms every day, so she's probably busy cleaning another floor. Was there something special you needed?"

"No," I said, slumping my shoulders. "I just wanted to give her an extra tip for the special housekeeping services she provided yesterday."

"You can leave it in an envelope on your pillow when you check-out of your room. I'll mention it to her, so she remembers to pick it up."

I wasn't sure if she was telling me the full truth, but I was far more concerned that I'd embarrassed Luna or somehow scared her from returning to my room. Had I come on too strong during our first encounter? Had I misread the signals that she seemed just as interested in me as I was with her? Had her manager admonished her for taking too long to finish my room?

For the rest of the day, I had a hard time concentrating on my client presentations, worrying that I'd lost my chance to reconnect with the sweet Latina beauty. I canceled my dinner plans hoping she'd return for my turndown service that evening, while flipping through the channels on my in-room TV to keep myself distracted. When I heard a soft tap on my door, I practically leapt off my bed, feeling my heart racing in excitement. I tiptoed to the door and peered through the peephole. I was delighted to see Luna standing there with another pretty girl about her same age, both dressed in casual clothes.

I swung open the door and peered at her inquisitively.

"I wasn't sure if I was going to see you again," I said, pinching my eyebrows in dismay.

"Sorry," Luna said, turning her head both ways to glance down the empty hallway. "It was my day off today, and I didn't want any of the other hotel staff seeing me entering your room. We're not supposed to mingle with the guests."

"Of course," I said, looking at her pretty companion. "Did you have any special plans? Would you like to go out for some drinks?"

"This is my friend Gabriella," Luna said. "She works with me at the hotel. Do you mind if I bring her along?"

"Of course not," I said, smiling at the other girl. "I just need a moment to freshen up before heading out. Would you like to come in while I get ready?"

"Sure," Luna said.

I stuck my head out the door to make sure it was clear, then I ushered the two girls into my room.

"I was afraid I might have scared you away after we met yesterday. The new maid wasn't entirely sure where you were."

"I'm sorry..." Luna hesitated. "I didn't have your number and I–"

I noticed the girls shifting their weight awkwardly in the narrow walkway next to my bathroom and I motioned them toward the side of my bed.

"Would you like to make yourselves comfortable while I straighten myself up?"

"Yes, thank you."

I went into the washroom to put on some lipstick and leaned over the sink, trying to see their reflection in the mirror. I had no idea why she'd decided to bring a friend, but my pussy twitched wondering if they might be lovers.

"I didn't catch your friend's name," I called from the bathroom.

"Gabriella," Luna said. "We started around the same time."

"At the hotel? What do you do, Gabriella?"

"I'm a waitress in the downstairs restaurant," she replied.

"You're both so pretty," I said. "I can only imagine how many times you get propositioned by lonely middle-aged travelers."

"It's not so bad," Gabriella said. "As long as we keep a healthy distance and don't flirt too much, we manage to stay out of trouble."

I smiled, remembering how easy it was to lure Luna into my bed.

"Have you known each other very long?" I said, fishing for more details about their personal relationship.

"Just a few months," Luna said. "We kind of hit it off right away."

I was intrigued why Luna would bring her friend to our second date, knowing how sexually charged it was likely to be. As I stepped out of the lavatory brushing my hair, I caught them inspecting my Rabbit vibrator as they giggled quietly between them. I guessed that they'd seen it sticking out from under the covers, and Luna must have been describing its various features. When she tried to stuff it back under the pillow, I held up my hand.

"Don't put it away on *my* account," I smiled. "Have you ever seen one of those before, Gabriella?"

"I Googled it after Luna told me about it," she said. "I've just seen what it looks like on their website."

"It's hard to appreciate it from a *picture*," I said, pulling it back out from under the covers and sitting down on the bed next to Gabriella. "Here, why don't you press some of the buttons and see for yourself."

I handed the purple dildo to her, and she fumbled with it awkwardly.

"Press the little button on the left-hand side of the controller," I said.

Gabriella tapped it, and the chrome beads began whirring in circles around the middle of the shaft. She jumped in surprise and looked up at me inquisitively.

"I bet you've never seen a boy's cock do *that* before," I smiled.

"Um, no..." she said, blushing softly.

"Try *this* one," I said, pointing to the button just below it.

When she tapped it, the penis-shaped head of the dildo began twisting like a spinning top and she almost dropped it in her lap.

"I *know*," I nodded. "If only *every* man could be equipped that way."

"What are these strange things on the side?" she said, pointing to the flexible rabbit ears.

"That's what *really* makes this special," I grinned, suspecting that Luna had already described the unique features of my vibrator in meticulous detail. I tapped the button on the bottom of the device, and the rabbit ears began flapping rapidly. "These two little fingers stimulate your clitoris while the rest of the vibrator is turning around inside you."

I peered up at Gabriella, then smiled at Luna.

"But you already *knew* that, didn't you? I'm sure Luna's already given you a full accounting of its various functions. You didn't just come here for a few *drinks*, did you?"

"Um..." Luna hesitated, peering over at her friend.

"It's okay," I said, taking the vibrator out of her hands and placing it on the nightstand next to my bed. "I'm glad you brought a friend. There's *so* many more ways we can enjoy this together."

I stood up and took off my clothes, throwing the pieces on the bed next to them, then pulled down the covers on the adjacent bed.

"You never know when double beds might come in handy on a business trip," I grinned.

While I stood in front of the two girls completely naked, they ran their eyes over my figure, lingering especially long at my glistening, hairless mound. Then I held out my hand to Gabriella and motioned for her to join me on the opposite bed.

"Come," I said. "Something tells me this isn't the first time you girls have experimented with sex toys. Let me show you how the *three* of us can make this a little more fun."

I lifted Gabriella off the bed, then pulled her turtleneck over her head and slowly unclasped her bra. Her breasts were smaller than Luna's, but rounder and firmer, with pink areolas and small button-shaped nipples. I cupped them gently, then leaned in to give her a wet kiss.

"You're beautiful, Gabriella," I gushed. "I can see why the two of you came together so quickly. I haven't seen such a pretty pair in a long time."

I peered down at her tight jeans, admiring the youthful contour of her hips.

"Do you need help getting out of those pants?"

"Yes please," she said as I watched her nipples contract and harden in excitement.

I reached down and unclasped the button at the top of her waistband, then lowered the zipper and pulled her jeans down to the floor as she kicked them off to the side. Then I kneeled down between her thighs and pulled her panties down to the floor, and she stepped out of them. Her bush was trimmed more neatly than Luna's, with a tawny amber color, and I leaned in to kiss it while I reached around and cupped her buttocks gently. Her ass quivered as I lowered my mouth to her moist slit, and she gasped when I circled her nub with my lips.

"Mmm," I moaned, as she pressed her mound harder into my face.

I peered out of the side of my eyes at Luna still sitting on the edge of the other bed, noticing her hand moving gently in her lap. The thought of her watching me while I ate out her best friend thrilled me, and I began to roll my hips unconsciously as I licked and teased Gabriella's burning clit.

"Uhnn," she grunted, spreading her legs further apart and angling her hips until she was standing directly over top of me. I squeezed her cheeks while her buttocks clenched together, and from the pace of her breathing I knew it wouldn't be long before she reached the peak of her pleasure.

I tilted my head up and watched her little boobs bouncing on her chest as she ran her fingers through my hair. She wasn't as aggressive as Luna had been holding me while I sucked her pussy, and I guessed that she was the submissive one in the relationship.

"Oh *God*," Gabriella suddenly moaned as she slumped over me, jerking her body in spastic movements.

I could tell from the intensity of her rocking motion that she was cumming on my face, and I held her tightly until she stopped moving. I pulled my head back and peered over at Luna, who had her knees spread wide apart and was rubbing her hand vigorously over a large stain in the crotch of her jeans.

"I think somebody *else* is missing out on all the fun," I said, shifting over and pulling her pants down over her curvy hips.

This time she'd chosen to go pantyless, and I looked up at her with a mischievous smile.

"Were you in a hurry to get started tonight?" I grinned.

"Going bare just reminded me of what it felt like to have you next to me," she smiled. "I didn't want anything else getting in the way."

I pulled her off the bed and ripped off her T-shirt, thrilled to see her oval-shaped melons bouncing freely on her chest.

"*Gawd*, how I've fantasized about these since I last saw you," I panted, pulling her toward me, mashing our bodies together. "But first, I had something different in mind."

I yanked the opposite bedspread all the way down toward the baseboard and instructed the two girls to kneel on the mattress, facing one another.

"I want to watch you enjoy my special vibrator together."

I handed the dildo to Gabriella and smiled.

"Why don't you place the long end inside, then press your bodies together so you can *both* enjoy the vibrating rabbit ears?"

Gabriella looked at Luna, and her friend nodded back at her.

"Knock yourselves out while I make myself more comfortable," I smiled.

I leaned back on my mattress and began circling my clit while I watched the two girls rubbing their bodies together. Gabriella tapped the buttons on the base of the unit and slowly inserted the oscillating device into her hole. She gasped in surprise at the unusual sensation, and Luna wrapped her arms around her shoulders, pulling their bodies together. As Gabriella began to thrust the humming vibrator in and out of her pussy, Luna pressed her mound against her girlfriend, purring in delight.

"Press the knob on the bottom now," I said to Gabriella, inserting two fingers into my slit.

Gabriella peered over at me, and her eyes widened as she watched me finger-fucking myself with my knees spread wide apart. She reached behind her ass and flexed her finger, and I heard a loud buzzing sound emanating from between their legs. The two girls groaned in pleasure as they felt the rabbit ears flapping against their joined clits, then they pressed their faces together, tonguing each other wildly. The image of the two sexy girls rubbing their bodies together as the big dildo whirled, twisted, and buzzed between both of their legs was surreal.

"*Fuck* yes," I hissed, ramming my fingers harder into my cunt. "Rub your tits and cunnies together while I watch you come."

"Mmm," Luna moaned, placing her hands over Gabriella's buttocks. "Come with me, Gabby," she said. "I can feel the rabbit ears touching both of our clits."

"Yes," Gabby whinnied, reaching around to grab Luna's ass at the same time. "I'm cumming, Lou. Oh *God*, I'm *cumming!*"

The two girls tilted their heads back and wailed in unison as their bodies began to quiver and tremble in simultaneous orgasm. I'd been so focused on watching them rubbing their bodies together that I'd barely paid any attention to what *I* was feeling, but the sight of them cumming together with my favorite vibrator purring between their legs quickly put me over the edge. I lifted my hips off the bed and thrust my fingers deep into my snatch and uttered a deep, guttural moan.

"Fuck *me*," I said, feeling my pussy clamp down hard over my fingers as my body levitated a foot above of the mattress. I held my body in this arched position for many long seconds while the three of us grunted and screamed in simultaneous ecstasy.

Suddenly I remembered where we were, and how thin the walls were between the adjoining rooms.

I wonder if all the other guests are expecting a similar type of turndown service, I smiled, flopping down onto the mattress in exhaustion.

6

When the girls lay down on the bed after coming down from their tandem orgasm, I nestled in next to them, and we cuddled silently for a few minutes. It felt incredible to have two gorgeous angels lying next to me as we nibbled and caressed each other's bodies, with nobody wanting to acknowledge what had just happened. But as they became progressively more daring in exploring my body, Luna pulled away and peered at her friend.

"I think it's *Jade's* turn now to get a little direct attention, don't you think Gabby?"

Gabriella nodded, and Luna turned her head toward me, lifting the Rabbit vibrator off the bed.

"How can we put this thing to work for all *three* of us?" she said. "We have too many body parts for one device to stimulate us at the same time."

I raised myself up on one arm and pushed the vibrator back down onto the mattress.

"I think each of us have had plenty enough stimulation from that thing. I'd far rather play with some flesh and blood pretty *girls* than have another cock inside me."

"Mmm," Luna grinned. "What can we do for *you* now that you've given us so much pleasure?"

I peered at Luna's tubular breasts and smiled.

"I've been fantasizing all day about you fucking me with those pretty melons. I want you to diddle me with your special tits."

"Okay," she said, lifting an eyebrow. "But what about Gabby? It seems such a waste for her to just stand by and *watch*."

I peered over at Gabriella and hesitated as I contemplated how to get all three of us involved at the same time. Then a huge grin slowly spread over my face.

"I have an idea," I said. "I'll lie down on the bed while Gabby straddles my face, as you lift up my hips and support me from behind. That way, you both can get a bird's-eye view of the action while I get serviced from both sides."

Luna's eyes opened wide as saucers as she pictured the scene in her mind.

"Holy shit," she said. "That will be so hot. Plus, we can *both* play with your pretty pussy from that position!"

"What are you waiting for?" I said, lying down with my ass pointed toward the headboard. "Come here little girl and sit on my face."

Gabriella got up on her hands and knees and placed her legs on opposite sides of my head facing Luna. As she slowly lowered her dripping pussy onto my face, Luna raised my hips off the bed and pressed her chest into my lower back until my body was perpendicular to the mattress. Then she spread her knees for support and pushed my legs apart. As my feet dangled in the air beside her shoulders, she grabbed one of her tits and pointed her erect teat toward my quivering hole. When I felt her flesh press against my vulva, I grunted into Gabriella's pussy writhing over my face.

"*Uhhn*," I groaned, unable to speak with my mind spinning in pleasure.

When Luna began rubbing her breast up and down my slit, I could hear the soft sloshing sound my pussy made as my labia puckered in and out in involuntary reflex. Although I couldn't see what she was doing with Gabby's ass buried over my face, the thought of them both looking at my upturned pussy drove me wild with pleasure.

Just when I thought it couldn't get any better, Gabby leaned forward and encircled my inflamed bud with her lips, rolling her tongue over my gland while she squeezed my tits. With her head now getting in the way of Luna's titfucking, her friend lowered her face down my perineum and began licking my freshly washed pucker.

I couldn't believe that every part of my body was now being serviced by these two angels, and I grunted in mounting ecstasy as my hips began to shake from my approaching orgasm. When it finally hit me, I growled like a wild animal while Gabriella pressed her pussy hard against my face and moaned along with me as she sucked my inflamed bean like a lollypop. When I felt Luna's tits rubbing against the back of my hips, my juices spurted out of me like a geyser, spraying all over both of the girls' faces.

I came for the longest time as the two girls held my body in this upright position, quivering and spurting while the entire length of my perineum flexed in powerful contractions. I wondered if Luna noticed my rosebud clenching in powerful contractions from her front-row seat immediately above my elevated pelvis. Either way, the thought of my most intimate parts exposed to their direct view as I came mere inches away from both of their faces magnified my arousal as I grunted under the weight of Gabby's trembling hips. When I finally stopped cumming, Luna lowered my hips back down onto the mattress and both girls lay beside me, caressing my drenched tits and abdomen.

"Oh my God," I panted, watching stars floating above my head as my mind spun in a drunken stupor. "That was even hotter than I imagined. I don't think I've come that hard in my entire life."

"We *noticed*," Luna smiled, wiping my juices off her face with the back of her hand. "You really opened the taps unexpectedly on the two of us."

"Sorry. I do that when I'm especially turned on. And I've never been stimulated like that before. That was incredible."

"We enjoyed it just as much as you did," Gabriella said, sucking my nipples softly into her mouth.

"Really?" I said, holding her head gently against my chest. "I couldn't tell with your hips buried on top of my face. Did you cum too? I didn't want to leave you hanging–"

"Oh, I *came* alright. Maybe not with the same degree of fireworks that you did, but when you started squirting all over my face, you opened the taps for me too. I've never been in a threesome before. Thanks for inviting me into your room."

I peered over at Luna and smiled.

"I think we have your friend to thank for that. I'm guessing this isn't the first time the two of you have had girl-on-girl sex before."

"No," Gabriella blushed. "But never quite like this."

7

———

"You know," I said, smiling at the two girls, realizing I had a once-in-a-lifetime opportunity. "We don't have a lot of time left before I have to leave town. We should make the best of our remaining time together."

"What else did you have in mind?" Luna said, propping herself up on an elbow.

"Everything we've done so far has been one-on-one, or just two girls enjoying each other's bodies. We still haven't had a chance for all *three* of us to come together yet."

Luna peered up at me and smiled.

"I have to confess that I was touching myself while I rubbed my breasts against your pussy," she said. "I came soon after I saw both of you climaxing."

"That makes me happy," I said, leaning in to kiss her moist lips. "But I was thinking of something even *more* interactive. Something where we all can be joined together at the same time."

The girls peered at me with a confused expression, shaking their heads.

"How is that even *possible*?" Gabriella said, pinching her eyebrows.

"With each of us having separate lady parts, how would we be able to touch them together simultaneously?"

"Surely you two have experimented with different types of *scissoring*?" I smiled.

"Yes..." Gabby blushed.

"Have you ever tried it *back-to-back*?" I said.

"How do you mean?" Luna said.

"I mean *ass-to-ass*. Two of us could rub our vulvas together, with the third one lying underneath as we ground our mounds together. I've never actually tried it, but I'm thinking it might work if we position ourselves the right way."

"I'm up for giving it a try," Luna smiled. "But who'll be on top and who'll be on the bottom?"

I looked at Luna and grinned.

"Something tells me you like to be the dominant one," I said. "Besides, I still haven't had quite enough of you. I've been dreaming about cunt-fucking you ever since I laid eyes on you. What do you say, Gabby? Would you like to have two sexy girls rubbing their pussies over top of you while you wrap your legs around our asses?"

"Oh my God," she gushed, turning her head toward Luna. "You weren't kidding when you told me about this crazy woman. I'm almost cumming just *thinking* about it!"

"It's *your* turn to lie down on the bed, girl," I instructed. "Would you like to take the inferior or superior position, Luna?"

Luna paused for a moment as she looked at me, trying to interpret my meaning. Then she nodded her head and smiled.

"I'll face her lower body, while you play with Gabby's tits. That way, I can watch her pussy twitching when we all come together."

"Works for me," I smiled, lifting my knee and placing my legs on opposite sides of Gabriella's hips.

Luna turned around and did the same thing, but with her head pointed toward Gabby's feet. We shifted our weight slightly backwards and when our asses touched, we arched our backs, angling our vulvas toward one another. When we felt our clits touch, each of us groaned.

"*Fuck*, yes," Luna hissed. "I want to feel you spray all over my ass when you come this time, Jade."

"My pleasure, hun," I said, peering into Gabby's eyes. "What do you say, Gab, are you ready to give this a try?"

"Damn *straight*," she said, pulling my head down and thrusting her tongue deep into my mouth.

As I swiveled my hips against Luna's ass and dripping pussy, I mashed my tits against Gabriella's chest, listening to her groan in my mouth. She tilted her hips and lifted her buttocks off the bed as I felt her grinding her mound against mine.

"That's it, baby," I purred. "Fuck my pussy while Luna tribs my ass. I'm going to spray all over your pretty cunny when I come."

"Mmm," Gabby moaned as I kissed her wildly.

The three of us were twisting our hips and grinding our pussies together, trying to find the right position where each of our clits received the ideal stimulation. I could feel Luna's labia intermingling with my own, and our pussies made nasty slurping noises as our asses smacked together. While our mutual passion escalated into a noisy cacophony of grunts and moans, Gabriella wrapped her arms and legs around my back and pressed her chest harder against my tits as she began to make funny squealing noises.

I knew she was close to cumming and as my *own* pleasure began to crest, I could feel it rushing toward me like a freight train. When the orgasm suddenly washed over me, the walls of my pussy suddenly clamped down hard and I began gushing all over Luna's bare ass and Gabby's pussy. Luna's buttocks began quaking next to mine as she howled in delight watching her girlfriend's vulva slapping open and shut in the throes of her own powerful climax. All three of us were climaxing now as we ground our pussies together in glorious union, grasping and clutching each other wildly. As we quivered, dripped, and squirted in mutual ecstasy for what seemed like an eternity, I suddenly became aware of how soaked the sheets had become.

It's going to be one hell of a clean-up operation for the next housekeeper,

I smiled. *But no matter—with the generous tip I plan to leave on my pillow when I check out, something tells me she won't mind.*

VOLUME THREE

THE HITCHHIKER

1

———

I 'd been looking forward to this trip for weeks. Normally, I flew to client meetings this far from home, but Des Moines was only four hours away by car. Factoring in check-in time at the airport, going through security, and taking taxis on both ends, it would take at least that long to travel there by plane. Plus, driving was infinitely less hassle. All I had to do was jump in my SUV, turn on the nav system, and point my way to my destination. All while soaking up the pretty midwestern scenery and listening to my favorite tunes on the radio.

Besides, I hadn't been on a road trip in years, and I was looking forward to feeling the sun on my face and the wind in my hair. There was something strangely romantic and liberating about the call of the open road. Being able to stop whenever you wanted, take a little detour if the mood struck, and watching the intoxicating flow of traffic like so many ants scurrying over their anthill.

After packing up a few days' worth of provisions and locking up my house, I turned out of my subdivision onto Route 30, heading west. This part of the trip was still familiar from my childhood forays into the lake district of northern Wisconsin, and I smiled as I breathed in the pastoral landscape of the passing farms. The countryside was a brilliant patchwork of yellows and greens, and my head lolled from side to side as I followed the neatly arranged rows of corn, soybeans, and wheat while my car glided down the two-lane highway.

After glancing down to dial in my favorite country music station, I looked up to see an unusual sight on the side of the road a few hundred feet ahead. It was something I hadn't seen for a long time–a hitchhiker. Curious to see who was still daring enough to catch a ride from a stranger in these troubling times, I squinted as the traveler came into focus. As the distance between us closed, my eyes widened when I realized it was a girl.

A young, scantily clad girl.

I could hardly believe my eyes as my car rushed past her. She couldn't have been more than eighteen years old, if that. Wearing tight, cut-off jean shorts and a white tank top, she had the young, nubile figure of a high-school teenager. My first reaction was one of shock and disbelief.

What in God's name is a girl like that doing thumbing a ride on the highway? Doesn't she realize how many predators are out there looking for an easy mark just like her?

As I watched her get smaller and smaller in my rear-view mirror, I shook my head disapprovingly, then suddenly screeched on the brakes and pulled over onto the shoulder. Normally I wouldn't give a second thought to taking on a hitchhiker knowing there was just as much risk for the driver, especially for a single woman like me. But there was something about this girl that I couldn't resist. Whether it was her naïve vulnerability or the appearance of her slender brown legs, I wasn't sure. Either way, the little twitch in my pussy told me this was an opportunity I couldn't pass up.

At first, she didn't notice that I'd pulled over, since I was so far ahead of her. I honked my horn and flashed my lights and she turned her head in my direction, then she picked up her small suitcase and began jogging toward me. Feeling sorry for her, I put my car in reverse and slowly backed up along the shoulder until we closed the gap. When she came up on my right side, I rolled down the passenger window and peered out at her.

"Where are you headed?" I smiled.

"California," she said, catching her breath.

"I'm only going as far as Des Moines, but I'm happy to point you in the right direction."

"Thanks," she nodded.

I unlocked my doors and tilted my head toward the back seat.

"You can throw your bag in the back if you want. But there's a lot more room up front to stretch your legs."

The girl opened the rear door and threw her carry-on-size roller bag on the back seat then climbed in the front next to me.

I smiled at her and checked my driver's mirror, then slowly pulled back onto the highway.

"I'm Jade," I said, introducing myself.

"Brooklyn," the girl replied.

"That's a pretty name. Do you go by Brooke, or Lynn, or do you like to be called by your full name?"

"Either way is fine. But most of my friends call me Brooke."

"Brooke it is," I nodded, interested to learn more about this mysterious stranger. "So, *California*? What's taking a pretty girl like you so far away from home?"

"I dunno," she said. "Just spreading my wings, I guess. Now that I've finished high school, I figured I might as well try my luck in La-La Land."

"Are you looking to be a movie star?" I laughed.

"Probably not. I thought I'd get a job as a waitress and check things out. But you never know, right? Wasn't that how Marilyn Monroe got discovered?"

I glanced over at the girl and smiled. With her curly blonde hair and piercing blue eyes, she could easily pass for a younger version of the matinee idol.

"Actually, I think she was working in a factory. But with those all-American looks, you've got as good a chance as any."

"Thanks," the girl said.

For the next couple of minutes, awkward silence filled the car as Brooke peered out her side of the window at the passing fields.

"It's pretty this time of the year, isn't it?" I said, making small talk. "I always like going for a drive as we approach harvest time. The crops are nearing full bloom, and you can smell the perfume in the air. Do you mind if I open the sunroof a bit so we can soak up the sunshine?"

"By all means," she said. "I probably should start working on my tan so I can keep up with all those California golden girls."

"I don't think you've got much to worry about," I said, glancing at her tawny thighs poking out of her cut-off jeans. There were so many questions I still had about this shy beauty. "But you're awfully young to be pulling up stakes and heading to the other side of the country. What do your parents think of this idea?"

"I'm not sure they much *care*," she shrugged. "My father lives in New York and my mother shacked up with an alcoholic who only seems to care where his next drink is coming from."

"I'm sorry to hear," I said, wincing at the thought of this pretty girl being neglected by uncaring parents.

"It's cool," she said. "I'm free as a bird now and the world is my oyster."

I peered over at Brooke, noticing her body language didn't match her cavalier attitude. She had her arms crossed tightly over her chest while her foot tapped nervously against the floorboard.

"Do they even *know* where you're headed?" I said. "I'm sorry to sound like an overbearing mother, but I'd hate for them to worry what happened to you."

"We had a fight earlier in the week when I told them I was thinking of leaving. My mother wanted me to go to college and my step-father just sees me as his meal ticket. I think he was afraid if I left that my mother wouldn't have any reason to keep him around."

I glanced over at Brooke and noticed a faint bruise around the base of her neck.

"But you *are* eighteen though? I mean, I wouldn't want to get either one of us in trouble..."

"Yes," she huffed sarcastically. "Just turned. I got the hell out of there just in time."

"Do you mind my asking why you weren't interested in going to college? You seem like a smart, well-spoken girl. Weren't your grades good enough?"

"I did well enough in high school," she said. "I just wanted to spread my wings before I get locked into another four years of school and a boring, dead-end job."

I couldn't help admire her free spirit and sense of adventure. But I wondered if there was another reason for her sudden uprooting.

"And there's nothing *else* keeping you close to home? Boyfriends, a steady job..."

"I've been saving up from my weekend job at Applebee's these last two years. Now I've finally got enough to start over on the west coast. I've had plenty enough of boys. They're only interested in one thing anyhow."

I felt my heart racing, seeing a window of opportunity opening. While I was in no hurry to take advantage of her, I felt like I'd found a kindred spirit. Even though there was fifteen years separating us in age, we shared a similar view on life with neither of us wanting to be held back by society's norms.

"Yeah, I know what you mean. My first husband wasn't exactly Mr. Perfect either. I'm in no hurry to jump into bed with another guy anytime soon."

I noticed Brooke's body language beginning to relax as she placed her arm on the door rest for support, hunching down a few inches in her seat.

"What are you headed to Des Moines for?" she asked.

"A meeting with a client. I'm a graphic designer and I'm going to review some ideas he had for updating his corporate identity."

"Corporate identity?"

"He operates a chain of restaurants. He wants to refresh his logo, menus, signage, and so on. It's a branding thing."

"Mmm," Brooke nodded. "Will you be staying long?"

"It's just a one-day meeting. But I've booked a hotel overnight so I'll be fresh for the drive back tomorrow."

Brooke peered back out the side of her window as we listened to the sound of the wind whistling through the overhead sunroof and soft country music on the radio. Periodically, I'd catch her stealing glimpses out the side of her eyes at my legs in my tight jeans and my loose blouse flapping in the breeze.

"Do you like your job?" she asked after a few minutes.

"It's a living," I said. "At least I'm my own boss and I get to exercise my creative juices. Each commission is different and I meet some interesting people along the way. How about you? Do you have any special passions or talents?"

"Not really. I was pretty good at science and math at school, but I can't think of a job in either of those fields that interests me."

I nodded my head, trying to think of a way to get her to open up a little more. So far, she'd played her cards pretty close to the vest, and I was beginning to wonder if there was any way I could draw her out of her shell.

"There's a lot you can do with those skills," I said. "Especially if you go on to college. Quite a few math majors move into finance. Quants make some big bucks on Wall Street. Trading, risk management, investment banking–maybe it would be an opportunity for you to reconnect with your father in New York?"

"He's got his own life now with a new bride and two toddlers. I'm not sure there's much room for me in his picture any longer."

"What about science?" I frowned. "There's so many interesting careers you could explore in that area. Marine biology, space exploration, you could even be a doctor."

"I'm too young to be thinking about all that mature stuff," Brooke said. "I've got my whole life ahead of me. There'll be plenty of time to explore my options when I settle down."

I peered over at Brooke, watching the breeze from the open sunroof swirling her blonde locks against her pretty face as she leaned back, closing her eyes.

"Sorry, I'm sure the last thing you want right now is to be stuck on a four-hour road trip with someone who sounds like your mother. No more career counseling, I promise. Let's just enjoy the open road and the wind in our hair!"

She issued a smile of relief, then I noticed her tapping her fingers on the edge of the door as she peered outside.

"Do you like Blake Shelton?" I said, seeing her foot tapping in rhythm to the music on the radio.

"He's fun to watch on The Voice. But I like this song. He and Gwen look like they really love each other in the video version."

"It sure is dreamy," I said, turning up the volume. "I'm not sure I'll ever find that kind of love."

While we listened to the song, Brooke began to hum the melody quietly under her breath.

"*I don't wanna look back in thirty years*," I sang along to the lyrics, trying to get her to open up. "And wonder who I'm married to..."

"*Wanna say it now, wanna make it clear*," Brooke joined in softly. "*For only you and God to hear...*"

"*When you love someone*," we joined in together, "*they say you set 'em free. But that ain't gonna work for me...*"

As the drumbeat introduced the chorus, I turned the volume up higher.

"*I don't wanna live without you*," we both belted. "*I don't wanna even breathe, don't wanna dream about you, wanna wake up with you next to me.*"

Brooke had a sweet, lilting tone, but I could see sadness in her eyes as she sang along with me. I smiled at her as I cranked the volume up until the beat surrounded us in the pounding cabin.

"*I don't wanna go down any other road now*," she sang, looking back at me. "*I don't wanna love nobody but you.*"

"*Looking in your eyes now*," we sang together. "*If I had to die now, I don't wanna love nobody but you...*"

As the song drifted off to the second verse, Brooke peered out her window, singing the rest of the song to herself. When I glanced over at her, I realized how vulnerable and alone she must have felt. I had no idea what kind of hardships she'd experienced in her young life, but from the pining sound of her voice, she looked broken and lost.

I peered ahead and saw a sign for a roadside rest area and looked over at her.

"Are you hungry?" I said. "There's an A&W restaurant at the pull-off. Nothing like a burger and fries with a down-home root beer to drown out your sorrows. My treat."

"Sure," Brooke said, smiling back at me. "I could go for a root beer right about now."

As I pulled off into the rest area, my heart skipped a beat. Somehow I knew this trip was going to have a lot more twists and turns than I planned.

2

------

rooke and I went inside the restaurant and waited in line while we decided what we wanted from the display menu behind the counter. I noticed a group of teenage boys in an adjacent line ogling her figure while they snickered and elbowed each other playfully. Whether they chose to keep their distance because they were too afraid to approach her or because they thought I was her mother, I wasn't sure.

But for the first time since I'd met her, I saw her up close from head to toe. Her ass was firm and well rounded, with the tight seam of her cut-off shorts separating her buttocks into two perfect circular globes. Her breasts weren't large, but they sat up prominently on her chest, pointing out like two snow cones under her form-fitting tank top. Her skin was soft and dewy like a teenager's, and golden brown with not a blemish to be found anywhere on her slender arms and legs.

As I admired her youthful, girl-next-door good looks, I understood why half the eyes in the room were checking her out.

If I was a teenage boy, I'd want a piece of that ass too.

I moved protectively beside her, and after we placed our order and collected our food trays, I found a booth in the far corner of the room. As she dug into her bacon and cheese burger, I watched the movement of her face while she peered back at me.

"What?" she said, gulping down her first mouthful. "Have I got mustard on my face or something?"

"No," I chuckled. "I was just thinking how a pretty girl dressed in such a skimpy outfit figured she could safely hitchhike her way all across the country."

"I don't know," she shrugged. "I've never done it before. But I figured the more skin I showed, the quicker I'd get picked up."

"That's for sure," I said, noticing the boys seated on the other side of the restaurant still stealing glances at her. "But you must know how attractive you are and how vulnerable you'd be to somebody who might have ulterior motives."

"I never really thought much about it, I guess," she said, dipping one of her fries in the cup of ketchup. "I was in such a hurry to get the hell out of my current abusive home, I just packed my bag and left."

"Is that what happened to your neck?" I said, glancing down at her bruise.

Brooke sat back on the bench and peered out the window pensively.

"My mom's boyfriend grabbed me there when I threatened to leave. Par for the course with that asshole."

I glanced at her and furrowed my brow, wondering what other indignities she'd suffered at the hands of the abusive lush.

"Did he abuse you in any *other* ways?"

"He tried often enough, but I got pretty good at reading the signs when he had too much to drink. I just made myself scarce until he sobered up."

"Now I see why you were so eager to leave," I nodded. "But you have to be careful that you don't trade one dangerous caretaker for another. There are a lot of ill-intentioned people out there just looking for an easy mark like yourself."

"I can take care of myself," she said. "I've made it this far on my own."

"Well, technically, you're less than one tenth of the way to Shangri La Land," I chuckled. "You've still got a long road ahead of you."

Brooke dipped another french fry into her ketchup, drawing some circles on the paper placemat lining her tray.

"As long as I'm careful whose car I get into, everything should be okay, right? There must be *lots* of other nice people like you out there willing to help a girl out."

"I suppose so, but you're rolling the dice with every new pick-up. It's unlikely you're going to find one person who'll take you the entire way."

"Maybe," she said, noisily sipping her root beer through her straw to distract attention from the conversation. "But tell me more about you. Do you have kids? Where do you live? Do you have any special plans for the future?"

"No kids," I laughed. "We barely had enough time to get started before our marriage disintegrated. I live in Naperville, just outside Chicago. As for the future, I'm just taking it day by day."

"You're not far from where *I* used to live in Aurora," Brooke said. "We're almost neighbors. What happened to your marriage, if you don't mind my asking. Why was it so short?"

"He wasn't very–*attentive*–to my needs," I said. "I guess it just wasn't everything I thought it was cracked up to be. You know, the knight in shining armor and all that."

"Like in that movie Pretty Woman?"

"Ha," I laughed, almost choking on my drink. "It was slightly different circumstances, but yeah, I guess I was expecting someone to sweep me off my feet and take me away to his castle to live happily ever after."

"No *other* worthy candidates since then?"

"I'm not really looking for that kind of relationship anymore. Like you said–I've had my fill of boys."

"Mmm," Brooke nodded, glancing down at the cleavage in my open blouse as she took another sip of her root beer.

For the rest of our lunch date, we teased each other about our inept experiences with men, giggling amongst ourselves at the juve-

nile attempts of the boys across the room trying to attract her attention. When we finished our meal, we skipped out into the parking lot
holding hands, then we jumped in the car and cranked up the music,
wailing together over the corny country songs. The time passed
quickly, and before I knew it, I saw the interchange approaching to
exit into Des Moines.

"Listen," I said, glancing at the clock on my dashboard. "I don't
feel right about just dropping you off at the side of the highway. Why
don't you come with me while I check into my hotel before I head off
to see my client? You can freshen up and watch a movie until I get
back. Then we can have dinner and you're welcome to stay with me
overnight before heading back out on the road tomorrow."

"Okay," Brooke said, nodding her head gently. "Thank you for
everything. For lunch, for picking me up–and for being such a good
listener. I can't imagine I'll find anyone who's half as much fun as you
to spend the rest of my trip with."

"Don't give it a second thought," I said, smiling back at her
warmly. "This has been an unexpected surprise for me too. You've
made my boring trip to Des Moines so much more interesting."

I took the second exit and drove to the downtown Marriott, then I
ordered a room with two double beds, and we carried our light bags
inside. After changing into my business clothes and straightening up
my lipstick and mascara, I handed Brooke one of the two room keys
I'd been given at the front desk.

"I shouldn't be more than a couple of hours," I said. "Why don't
you make yourself comfortable while I'm away. Feel free to order a
movie and charge any meals to the room. But whatever you do, stay
far away from the single men you find in the hotel. You'd be the
perfect distraction while they're away from their wives back home."

"Don't worry," Brooke laughed. "I'll stay right here until you get
back. Good luck at your meeting."

"Thanks, hun," I smiled. "See you soon."

For the rest of the afternoon, I had a hard time concentrating at my meeting with my client. All I could think about was Brooke's pretty face and the look she gave me when I left the room. Even though there was a wide gulf in age between the two of us, I found myself strangely attracted to the free-spirited girl and I was eager to get back to her as quickly as I could. I felt much more than a mother-and-daughter-type bond; my head was spinning and my stomach had butterflies, like I had a teenage crush. Which I suppose it *was*, in a strangely perverted way. Although the periodic twitching in my pussy told me this was a decidedly *grown-up* infatuation.

When my client invited me out for dinner at the close of our meeting, I politely declined, using the excuse of wanting to visit family members in town. I rushed back to my hotel, hoping Brooke hadn't gotten second thoughts about staying with me for the evening, as I fumbled awkwardly with my room key outside the hotel room door. When I swung it open, I was relieved to see her sitting upright on one of the beds, watching the movie Pretty Woman while munching on a large bag of Cheesies.

"I was afraid maybe you wouldn't *be* here when I got back," I said, throwing my briefcase on the opposite bed.

"Of course I'd be here," she said. "Why would I throw away this free meal ticket?"

I glanced at the TV and smiled.

"I see you've made yourself comfortable. Have you been fantasizing about finding your knight in shining armor?"

"Maybe," she said. "Although Richard Gere isn't exactly my type."

"Oh?" I said, hoping to get more hints about her sexual persuasion. "Who *is* your type?"

"I dunno," she said. "I'm still figuring it out. But it seems to be rapidly morphing away from the Tom Cruise leading man prototype."

"He's too short for you anyhow," I laughed, recognizing a familiar scene in her movie. "I love this part when Richard Gere's character pulls up in his stretch limousine and begs Julia Roberts to run away with him."

Brooke peered up at me then patted the bed beside her.

"Why don't you come join me while we finish the movie together? Do you like Cheesies?"

I laughed as I kicked off my leather pumps and threw my suit jacket on the bed.

"I haven't had them in ages, but yeah, they used to be one of my favorite guilty pleasures."

I plopped myself down on the bed beside Brooke, and we watched the rest of the movie side-by-side as we noisily crunched on the cheesy snack. When it was finally over, we looked at our orange-crusted fingers and giggled.

"*Ew,*" Brooke said, scrunching up her face. "I can't believe we ate that whole bag in one sitting. I've got to wash myself up before I get this all over everything."

While Brooke disappeared into the washroom, I cleaned my hands with wet wipes from my purse, then I changed out of my work clothes back into my jeans. When she emerged a few minutes later, she peered at my new ensemble and smiled.

"I like this look better on you," she said. "You look less like my mother and more like my partner-in-crime."

"Like *Thelma and Louise*?" I smiled. "God forbid that I'd remind you of your mother."

"I don't think there's any danger of that," she said, checking my figure out like I was with her at the restaurant.

"Are you up for a proper dinner after eating all that junk food?" I said, changing the subject. "I could go for a nice steak and a glass of wine right about now."

"Absolutely," Brooke said. "Although I'll have to pass on the wine, unless Iowa has a lower drinking age than Illinois."

"Oh yeah," I said. "I keep forgetting how young you are. I'm sure we can find something else to keep you amused. Maybe they can scare up a Shirley Temple or something like that."

"Ha!" Brooke said, placing her hands on her hips in mock protest. "I'm not *that* young!"

We took the elevator down to the lobby, then I asked at the front desk for the location of some good nearby restaurants. After enquiring about Brooke's food preferences, we decided on the Outback Steakhouse. When we were seated at the restaurant, I ordered a top sirloin steak with a glass of cabernet and Brooke ordered the pork ribs and a Coke. As we dug into our meals and talked about our favorite movies, I kept staring at Brooke's pretty face smeared with BBQ sauce, imagining it was my pussy juices instead of the tangy marinade.

"You're giving me that *look* again," she said, noticing me staring at her lips.

"It's just that you seem to have a propensity for finger food and getting your fingers messy while you eat."

"Hey, I'm a *teenager!*" she protested. "You can go ahead and eat your old-people food all prim and proper with a knife and fork. I'm gonna enjoy my pizza and burgers and fried food all I like."

"Who are you calling *old*?" I said, raising an eyebrow.

"Well you're older than *me*, aren't you? You've already been married and divorced, holding down a boring day job, driving an old person car–"

"It's not an *old person's* car," I said. "And I'm not boring, I'm just–*responsible*. Something you'd do well to learn before you end up living in the streets or get picked up by some sugar daddy."

"I didn't *ask* for all this," she said, twirling her finger sarcastically in the air while peering around the restaurant. "I was doing just *fine* before you plucked me off the highway."

I swallowed my mouthful with a lump in my throat as I digested what had just happened. Somehow, we'd gone from laughing about our favorite movies to disparaging each other's life choices. My heart began racing a million miles an hour, shocked that we'd had our first fight after barely knowing each other for one day.

For the rest of the meal and the drive back to the hotel, we hardly said a word to one another as we stared out our windows, fuming. But the tightness in my stomach told me this was more than just a minor quarrel. People didn't get this passionate about issues and this angry at one another unless there was already some strong feelings between them. But mostly, I was afraid that I'd lost Brooke and that she'd use this as an excuse to run away again.

When we got back to the hotel, we took the elevator silently back up to our room then Brooke kicked off her sneakers, pulled her bra out from under her tank top and she climbed under the covers of her bed, sulking. I took a few minutes to brush my teeth and remove my makeup, then I pulled on a t-shirt and got into my bed wearing only my panties. As we both lay on the bed staring up at the ceiling, we could hear each other breathing mere inches away.

My mind raced thinking about what I should do with this young girl who'd I'd grown so close to in such a short period of time. I dreaded the idea of driving back home tomorrow without her, but I was far more worried about her continuing on her way by herself. After this new flare-up, I began to wonder if it wasn't for the best for the two of us to part company cleanly.

After a long pause, Brooke was the first to break the silence.

"I'm sorry, Jade, she said. "I didn't mean what I said about you being old and boring. I actually think you're one of the coolest, prettiest, and smartest persons I've met in a long time."

I paused for a long moment, feeling my heartbeat returning to normal.

"And I didn't mean what I said about your being irresponsible. I admire your free spirit and independence. I wish I were as courageous as you when I was your age."

For the next two hours, we talked about our dreams and aspirations, joking about our lost loves and missed opportunities. By the time I drifted off to sleep, I felt much more comfortable about the strength of our fledgling relationship. But a few hours later, I woke to the sound of rustling next to me in the pitch black. Brooke was shifting her weight erratically under her bedsheets, and I held my breath trying to listen to what she was doing.

After a few minutes, it became apparent from her raspy breathing and the rhythmic rustling of her sheets that she was masturbating under the covers. I could hardly believe what I was hearing, and my panties filled with moistness as I got more and more turned on listening to her pleasuring herself. She tried to be as quiet as she could, but the unmistakable ratcheting of her breath and the faster rustling of her sheets left little doubt that she was nearing climax. Suddenly, I could see her lifting her hips off the bed in the soft moonlight filtering through the crack in our curtains while she gasped in staccato succession.

Fuck me, I thought, squeezing my thighs together quietly under my covers. *That is the hottest thing I've ever heard in my life.*

I wasn't sure if her sudden arousal was because she was lying next to me in the quiet hotel room and she felt attracted to me, or if it was simply her teenage hormones taking control. Either way, there was no way I was going to be able to get back to sleep after that, and I waited until I heard her breathing returning to normal and she rolled over in her bed.

When I was sure she'd fallen back to sleep, I pulled down my panties and began jilling myself in furious circles over my burning clit. After getting so worked up listening to her touching herself, it didn't long for me to reach the peak of my pleasure. I bit my lip trying to stifle my groans as my body began convulsing in rhythmic contractions with my hand pressed tightly between my legs. When I finally stopped coming, I tried to control my breathing so as not to wake Brooke up. But when she suddenly rolled over again, I wondered if it was because she was restless or because she'd been listening to me the whole time.

Either way, I knew we'd both passed an important milestone in our mutual journey of discovery.

3

———

I n the morning, Brooke woke up before me and went into the washroom to brush her teeth. My panties were still damp from my late-night masturbation session, and I was eager to get myself cleaned up before heading out. I sat up on the edge of my bed to check my messages, but it was all a blur as my mind raced thinking about what to do next. I couldn't bear the idea of leaving Brooke, but I had my life in Chicago and she was dead-set on traveling to LA. As I contemplated how to reconcile my conflicting urges, she stepped out of the washroom and paused in the doorway.

"Did you sleep well?" she asked.

I peered up, seeing the raised bumps of her areolas protruding atop her perky breasts under her braless tank top.

"Um, yes thank you," I stammered, momentarily taken aback by her sexy Elizabeth Taylor pose. "How about you?"

"Better than I have in a long time. Must be all this fresh midwestern air."

"That, or us staying up so late. What time do you figure we nodded off?"

"I dunno, but I enjoyed chatting with you into the wee hours. I haven't had that much fun since my grade school sleepovers."

"Everything but the pillow fight," I chuckled, alluding to our silent late-night tryst.

"Mmm," she nodded, flushing slightly.

I stood up and picked my toiletry bag out of my suitcase lying on the bench at the base of my bed.

"I need a shower. You'll probably want one too before heading back out on the road. You don't know when you might have the next opportunity. Do you want to go first?"

Brooke peered at my full breasts pressing against the flimsy cotton of my t-shirt. They were bigger than hers, and my erect nipples poked two sensuous darts in the light fabric. As I approached her near the entrance to the bathroom, she peered into my eyes and we hesitated for a moment. I was tempted to lean in and kiss her, but it still felt too soon. Besides, I didn't know if I was ever going to see her again. The last thing I needed was to get my pheromones all worked up again, only to be dashed when she sailed off into the sunset.

"No," she said, feeling our breasts only inches apart in the narrow doorway. "You go first. I'm going to check the highway route map to see the best place to pick up on my journey."

"Mmm," I nodded, not wanting to broach the subject that was on both of our minds. I could tell that neither of us was in any hurry to separate, but we were both painfully aware of the reality of the situation.

I continued into the washroom, closing the door partway behind me. Then I stepped out of my panties and pulled off my t-shirt, bending over to adjust the shower temperature. When I stood up to step into the tub, I caught Brooke peeking at me through the narrow crack, and she quickly turned away, pretending to thumb through her phone.

As I stepped into the warm shower feeling the soft spray caressing my bare tits and stomach, I flashed back to the scene from last night. Remembering the way Brooke raised her hips off the mattress and mewed when she came made my pussy tingle, and I snaked my hand between my legs and began to play with my nub. Within seconds, I had another powerful orgasm as I jerked and panted, trying to support myself with one hand against the slippery wall. When I finished washing my hair and cleaning my body, I stepped out of the tub and wrapped a towel around my torso and another around my wet hair. Then I opened the door as a rush of warm humid air spilled into the bedroom.

"Your turn," I said, smiling at Brooke. "I hope you don't mind that I took a couple of towels. There's still one large bath towel and a hand towel for you to use. You can borrow my hair dryer if you forgot to pack one."

"Thanks," Brooke said, slipping past me into the washroom. "Do you mind if I leave the door slightly ajar so as not to steam up the mirror?"

"I was thinking exactly the same thing," I smiled back at her.

Brooke closed the door partway then I heard the rustling of clothes as she disrobed, followed by the sound of the shower curtain being pulled back. When I heard the spray turn on, I peered up and saw her naked body briefly exposed in the mirror over the sink from my angle on the bed. Her tits were soft and round, like two bowls of Jello resting high on her chest, with pointy nipples that danced in the warm spray.

Oh, to be eighteen years old again, I thought as my pussy pulsed in unconscious spasms.

When she got out of the shower, she wrapped the bath sheet around her body and we took turns drying our hair with my blow dryer. Brooke left hers purposely damp to let it dry with a natural curl, and when she emerged from the bathroom, she reminded me of Kristen Stewart in the famous river scene from the finale of the Breaking Dawn Twilight movie. We got dressed separately in the privacy of the washroom, then we headed downstairs for a quick breakfast in the hotel restaurant before checking out.

After collecting a plateful of bacon and eggs from the breakfast bar, we sat down at our table and ate quietly together. Neither one of us wanted to acknowledge the elephant in the room. After a couple of minutes of awkward silence, I put my fork down on my plate and peered up at Brooke.

"Listen," I said. "I've been thinking. There's nothing urgent I need to rush home to for a few more days. Why don't I take you a little further along the way toward your destination? We can make a little adventure of it. Stop at Mount Rushmore, see the Grand Canyon, stuff like that."

"Like *Thelma and Louise*?!" she said, her eyes suddenly widening in excitement.

"Yes, everything except the driving over the cliff part at the end. That is, if you don't mind being seen in an *old person* car."

"I dunno," Brooke grinned. "It's a far cry from the Thunderbird convertible that Louise drove. But hey, beggars can't be choosers."

I lifted my glass of orange juice off the table and pointed it toward Brooke.

"Here's to new adventures," I said.

"To new adventures," she nodded, clinking her glass against mine.

After we packed our bags in the back of my SUV, Brooke turned toward me and wrapped her arms around my neck, giving me a bear hug.

"Thanks, Jade," she said. "I couldn't bear the idea of going the rest of the way without you. I feel like I've known you my whole life after being with you for only one day."

"Don't get your hopes up *too* far, young lady," I smiled. "I didn't promise to drive you the whole way. We'll take it day by day and see how far we can make it without getting into another fight."

"*Deal*," Brooke said, clapping her hands together excitedly.

We jumped in the car and after reaching the outskirts of Des Moines, I pulled back onto I-80 West, before angling northward toward Sioux Falls in South Dakota. We marveled at the passing landscape as the highway wound its way along the banks of the

Missouri River, singing country songs the entire way while our hair flapped in the wind outside our open windows.

When we got to Mount Rushmore, we picnicked in the grass at the base of the mountain, then took selfies with the four presidents peering over our shoulder. I mimicked the serious expressions of Lincoln, Jefferson, Washington, and Roosevelt, while Brooke made funny faces, sticking her tongue out the side of her mouth as she rolled her eyes. I hadn't laughed and had so much fun for as long as I could remember, and for the first time in ages, I lost track of what day of the week it was. We were just following our noses, letting the car take us wherever it wanted as we pointed west.

I felt my heart soaring with every new mile we traveled, feeling closer and closer to this free-spirited girl. But it was more than just a strong friendship. I lusted to be in Brooke's arms, to feel her body pressed against mine as I ravished her and we pleasured each other to new heights. After our silent tryst the night before, I was afraid to make the next move, not knowing if she was ready for an intimate relationship with a woman.

As we continued across the midwestern plains into Wyoming, Brooke seemed to become more and more restless and she began to shift in her seat distractedly. Suddenly, she popped open the glove box and reached inside.

"Have you got any *good reading* material in here?" she said. "There's only so many cornfields a girl can watch before she needs a diversion."

"Um–not really," I hesitated, remembering something *else* I kept stored in the stowage compartment.

Brooke felt something hard with her hand and began pulling it out of the box.

"What's this?" she said. "Do you keep a gun in here, just like Louise? Were you planning on running into some dangerous characters along the way?"

"Ah–" I stammered, unsure how to stop her.

"*Holy shit!*" she said, holding up my special vibrator that I carried to keep me amused on long trips. "Is this what I *think* it is?"

"Um…"

"It *is!*" Brooke squealed, squeezing the soft silicone covering. "But I've never seen one like this before. Why is it shaped like a horseshoe?"

"It's a special type of vibrator," I smiled. "One that stimulates you on the inside and the outside at the same time."

"Really?" Brooke hummed. "You actually *use* this thing sometimes when you're driving?"

"Only when I'm especially bored or I feel drowsy on long trips. It certainly keeps me awake."

"I can imagine," Brooke said, gently flexing the two sides of the U-shaped device. "I've never used one like this before."

I smiled, happy to know she'd had a little experience using vibrators.

"You haven't *lived* until you've tried this one. You said you were looking for a distraction. Why don't you give it a try?"

"What—right *here*? Right *now*?"

"Why not? It's just us girls. No one will be able to see what you're doing this far under the windowsill."

"Except *you*. You're sitting right next to me."

"I promise not to look if you don't want me to. Besides, I need to keep my eyes on the road."

"Um," Brooke hesitated, beginning to squirm in her seat.

I could tell she was curious about giving it a try, but her modesty was holding her back.

"Here," I said, reaching into the back seat to retrieve her small travel bag. "Why don't you rest this on the console between the two of us. That will give you a certain degree of privacy. I won't be able to see much below your upper body that way. If you insist on being discreet."

Brooke hesitated for a moment, then peered over her shoulder into the back seat.

"I can't believe I'm actually thinking of doing this. But now you've piqued my curiosity."

"You could always wait until later tonight when the lights are out in our hotel room," I smiled.

"Very funny," Brooke grinned back at me. "I think I'll try it here. I'm going to enjoy teasing you while your hands are tied up on the wheel. No peeking though, okay?

"I promise," I said. "Not unless you want me to."

Brooke lifted her travel bag between the two front seats and placed it on the dividing console. It wedged snugly between the two seats, and the gearshift kept it from sliding forward.

"Okay," Brooke said, peering over the top of the bag at me. "No cheating."

"Yes ma'am," I said, squeezing the steering wheel so tightly in anticipation that my fingers began to turn red.

Brooke reached down with her hands and wiggled her hips as she pulled her cut-off shorts and panties down around her ankles. Then she lifted up the U-shaped vibrator and peered at it curiously.

"Which end goes *inside*?"

"The fat end that's curved like a finger. I think you'll find it does quite a nice job of stimulating your G-spot. Then you place the narrower, flat end against your mound and push it all the way inside until it rests against your vulva. Do you need some *lube*? There's a small jar inside the glove–"

"No need," Brooke smiled. "I'm plenty lubricated already."

She spread her legs, and I saw the muscles of her arms tense as she pressed the device slowly inside her with two hands. She purred softly, then gasped when the soft outer tip rolled over her clitoris.

"Mmm–it feels heavenly," she purred. "But how do I turn it on?"

"That's the most fun part," I said, grinning back at her. "If you reach into the glove box, you'll find a separate attachment in the shape of a pink disk. It's a remote controller–so you can use it completely hands free."

Brooke placed her hand into the glove box and pulled out the strange-looking device, rubbing her fingers over the various indentations.

"There's a lot of buttons and switches on this thing," she said. "Which button controls which part?"

"You know what would be even *more* fun," I grinned. "Is if you let *me* operate the controls. That way, you can just put your head back and enjoy the ride."

"But I thought you said you needed to keep your eyes on the road?!"

"Oh, I can operate these controls entirely by *feel*, believe me. I've had plenty of practice."

"Okay," Brooke said, slowly handing me the controller overtop of the console. "But if I tell you to slow down or stop, you have to follow my instructions. I don't want you giving me a seizure or something."

"I wouldn't think of it," I smiled. "Are you ready?"

"I guess so," she said, tilting the back of her seat down a few inches and closing her eyes.

I tapped the lower control button once and I heard the vibrator begin to hum inside Brooke's pussy. She groaned as she wedged her body further down the seat, spreading her legs wider apart. I smiled, knowing the internal finger had begun to move slowly inside her.

"Good so far?" I said.

"Mmm, yes," she said, squirming in her seat. "More, please."

I tapped the lower button two more times, and the speed and motion of the internal wand ramped up in intensity.

Brooke groaned softly as her right hand gripped the handle on the side of her door.

"You *like*?" I said.

"Oh yes–very much," she mewed, beginning to move her hips in rhythmic circles on the leather seat. "But what about the *outside* part? I can't feel it moving yet."

"Are you sure you can handle it?" I teased.

"*Fuck* yes," she groaned. "I need you to stimulate my clit."

I squeezed my legs together in my tight jeans, getting increasingly turned on by the sights and sounds of Brooke's mounting arousal. I gripped the disk tightly in my right hand while trying to keep my eyes glued ahead, but my vision kept drifting to my right the more worked up Brooke became.

"Okay," I said. "Here goes."

I tapped the upper button on the controller, then I heard a higher-pitched sound as the clitoral vibrator began to buzz against Brooke's mound.

"Oh *God*," Brooke moaned, gripping the door handle more tightly. "That feels incredible."

I glanced over at her upper body and saw her chest beginning to rise and fall as her breathing became more ragged. Suddenly I wished she'd chosen to go braless again under her tight tank top as I flashed back to the memory of her pretty tits pressing against the soft fabric.

"Mmm," I encouraged her, rubbing my thighs tighter together, feeling the seam of my crotch pulling up harder against my throbbing button.

"Do you want more?" I asked, peering over at her.

"There's *more*?" she said, looking at me incredulously.

"I can turn up the speed a bit higher if you think you can take it."

"Oh, I can *take* it, alright," Brooke panted.

I tapped the upper button twice more, and the clitoral vibrator began buzzing at a higher pitch and faster intensity.

"*Uhnn*," Brooke groaned, shifting further down in her seat and spreading her legs further apart until her knees pressed against the sides of the footwell.

"Damn," she grunted. "I can't take this much longer. You're enjoying tormenting me, aren't you?"

"You have *no* idea," I purred, feeling my own pleasure rising from the friction of my seam against my burning clit.

"Oh God," she suddenly panted. "I'm gonna cum. I'm gonna come so hard–"

She lurched forward, jerking her torso in rhythmic movements as her legs flapped rapidly in and out.

"Oh *fuckkk*!" she hissed. "I'm cumming, Jade! *Uhnnn...*"

As I watched Brooke spasming in her seat from her powerful

climax, a switch suddenly flipped in my body, and I grunted softly as my own silent orgasm washed over me. I was oblivious to the traffic rolling past us in both directions as my vision blurred from the intense pleasure I was feeling, knowing the two of us had achieved a new level of intimacy in our rapidly blossoming relationship.

I smiled, realizing this was another unexpected turn in our open-ended adventure.

4

———

After Brooke came down from her climax, she wiped down the vibrator then placed it back in the glove box. I was hoping she'd play with it a little longer or dare me to use it while I was driving, but it was starting to get late and we needed to find a place to put in for the night. Hotels were scarce in the eastern part of Wyoming, so we pulled into a run-down motel and I booked another room with two double beds.

After checking for any sign of bedbugs, I told Brooke to make herself comfortable while I searched for some takeout food. I had to drive ten more miles to find a fast-food outlet in the nearest town, and after picking up a bucket of fried chicken, I stopped off at the liquor store to buy a bottle of wine. I hoped that one or two glasses in the privacy of our own room might loosen Brooke's inhibitions about taking our relationship to the next level.

But when I stepped into the store, I immediately felt uncomfortable, surrounded by a bunch of middle-aged truckers and noisy rednecks wearing dirty baseball caps and greasy mullets. They leered at me as I stepped into the checkout line, and I was happy to get out of there and back to the relative safety of our little motor hotel.

But when I pulled into the parking lot, I saw Brooke standing outside our door flanked by two young men who were pushing her against the wall, trying to grope her. I could tell from the look in her eyes that she was frightened, and I screeched the brakes, pulling up directly in front of them.

"*Hey!*" I yelled, swinging my car door open and grabbing the paper bag with the bottle of wine. "*Get away from her!*"

"Who's this?" one of the punks said, gripping Brooke's arm while he pressed his face closer to hers. "Is this your Mommy coming to save you from the big bad wolf?"

Brooke shook her head apprehensively while pressing herself further back against the wall.

"What do you want, *bitch*?" the boy said, teetering unsteadily and obviously drunk. "Can't you see I'm busy? Why don't you mind your own business and lose yourself in your bottle of wine? Or better yet, share it with *us*."

As he lurched toward me, without thinking, I coiled back and gave him a hard kick to the side of his knee. He howled in pain from the torn ligament and crumpled to the ground. His friend stepped toward me threateningly, and I crashed the end of the bottle against my side mirror as wine spilled out onto the pavement and jagged glass jutted out the end of the torn bag.

"You want some of this too?" I scowled, pressing the sharp glass up close to his face. "I won't hesitate to cut you up like a tree chipper if you get any closer."

The boy looked at me for a moment, then peered down at his fallen comrade, still squirming in pain on the ground.

"Come on, Bo," he said, reaching down to help him off the pavement. "This bitch is bat-shit crazy, and that tramp ain't worth it. Let's get the hell out of here before someone calls the cops."

The boy on the ground staggered to his feet and began limping away, when I noticed a bulge in the back pocket of his jeans. I reached in and pulled out his wallet, flipping through the contents.

"What the *fuck*?" the boy said. "Give me back my wallet or I'll call the cops!"

I pulled out his driver's license, then threw his wallet back down on the ground.

"You can *have* your wallet," I said. "But I'm keeping your ID in case you two get any ideas about coming back here anytime soon. Feel free to call the police. We'll see who gets taken to the station house. I'll leave your license at the front desk when I check-out. Now get the fuck out of here!"

The injured boy placed his arm over his friend's shoulder then they limped to the other side of the parking lot and got into an old Camaro, squealing their tires out of the compound.

Brooke peeled herself off the wall and looked at me incredulously.

"Holy shit, Jade!" she said. "That was *bad-ass!* Where did you learn those moves?"

"Just reflex, I guess. The adrenaline was pumping pretty hard when I saw what they were doing to you. Are you alright?"

"Yes," she said. "It's mostly just my pride that was injured." She peered down at the broken bag of wine, still dripping onto the black-top. "It's a good thing you brought that bottle of wine. That scared them away right quick!"

"Sorry," I said, throwing the bag into a trash receptacle near our door. "I was hoping we could share a little together to celebrate reaching your halfway point."

"No worries," Brooke said. "There'll be plenty more opportunities along the way. Did you pick up some food? I've been starved since our picnic earlier in the day."

I opened the rear driver's side door and pulled out the bag of KFC.

"Fried chicken," I smiled. "Your favorite!"

We went inside the cabin and spread a towel over one of the beds, then we sat cross-legged on the mattress facing one another while Brooke replayed the scene outside.

"What were you *thinking?*" I said, peering at her with pinched eyebrows. "What prompted you to leave the room?"

"I just wanted to get a soda from the pop machine near the lobby. I didn't see the two goons until it was too late."

"It's okay, babe," I said, placing my hand on her still-quivering shoulder. "You've got to be careful out there. Like I said, there's a lot of scary people just waiting to take advantage of a single girl like you."

"Don't worry," she smiled guiltily. "I'm not going *anywhere* without you from now on."

After we finished eating and cleaning up in the washroom, I peered at Brooke and smiled.

"Are you ready to turn in? It's getting pretty late. Do you think you'll be able to sleep after all this?"

Brooke stood next to her bed with her arms crossed tightly over her chest, still shaking visibly.

"Do you mind if I sleep with you tonight?" she said. "I'll feel safer having a warm body next to me."

"Of course," I smiled, turning down the covers of my bed. "There should be enough room for the two of us."

As I pulled off my jeans and draped them over the back of the chair, Brooke stepped out of her cut-off shorts and threw them on top of the opposite bed.

"You might want to put those somewhere *else*," I said. "I'm guessing that bedspread hasn't been washed in months. You never know what kind of germs might be lurking in this place."

"Right," she said, lifting her shorts off the bed and placing them atop my jeans on the back of the chair. Then she pulled her bra down under her shirt and placed it cup-side-up on top of her shorts. I followed suit, then we both lay down on the bed wearing only our cotton shirts and panties.

After I turned out the night table lamp, Brooke nestled in closer to me, squeezing her body against mine.

"Thanks, Jade," she whispered in my ear. "I feel so lucky to have found you. And not just because you saved me today. There's something else. I've never felt this way with–"

I placed my hand at the side of her head and pulled her face into mine, kissing her gently. She mewed like a kitten while pressing her hips against me, grinding her mound against mine. I pulled her head harder toward me and slipped my tongue into her mouth, teasing the inside of her lips. She moaned as she wrapped her arms around my back, pressing her tits against mine.

I pulled back for a second and peered into her eyes in the faint light projected by the digital clock on the desk.

"Are you sure you want to do this?" I asked. "I don't want to take advantage–"

"I've been wanting you to make love to me ever since we had that fight in the restaurant. Haven't you felt the sexual tension too?"

"Yes," I said, kissing her softly. "I've just been looking for the right moment–"

Brooke leaned back a few inches and pulled off her tank top then threw it over her shoulder onto the opposite bed.

"Aren't you worried about the *germs*?" I said.

"Not *those* ones," she smiled. "I'm looking forward to intermingling with some *other* organisms."

"Mmm," I said, pulling off my t-shirt and throwing it on top of hers.

Brooke threw her arms around me, mashing her tits against mine as we moaned into each other's mouths. I could tell from her awkward movements that this was her first time with a woman, and I decided to go slow so as not to scare her away. Normally, I'd have started kissing my way down her body by now, sucking her teats and clit into my mouth as I indulged her with my more experienced skills. But right now, I just wanted to feel her body against mine while I kissed her sweet face. There'd be plenty more time to get down and dirty after a good night's sleep.

As the two of us intertwined our legs and began rubbing our pussies together, I could feel my panties getting wetter and wetter as the lacy fabric pulled and scratched against my skin. I reached down under the covers and began pulling Brooke's panties down over her hips, and she lifted her knees up and kicked them off her feet. I raised my hips off the mattress and did the same thing, pushing the two pairs of panties out of our way down toward the base of the bed.

Then I pressed my knee between her legs and pulled my thigh up toward her crotch. I was surprised how wet she was already, and I groaned when I felt her warm pussy against the soft skin of my upper leg. As I began rocking my thigh over her dripping vulva, she sighed in my ear while nibbling my earlobe.

"Make love to me, Jade," she whispered. "I want to feel your body against mine while I listen to you in the dark again."

I pulled away and smiled into her eyes.

"So you *did* hear me last night after all?" I said, flaring my eyes in mock surprise.

"Of course," she said. "Did you hear me?"

"How could I *not*? With all that shuffling and heavy breathing, I knew immediately what you were up to."

"Did that turn you on?" she said.

"Damn straight," I said, rolling on top of her. "You have no idea how much I've fantasized about fucking you since then."

"Mmm," Brooke groaned, feeling my bare mound rubbing up against her soft muff. "Fuck me, Jade. I want to feel your juices dripping over my pussy."

"*God* yes," I panted, pressing her legs apart with my knees and positioning myself over her upper body as our sweaty tits slid effortlessly over one another.

Brooke tilted her hips up a few degrees until her clit made contact with the base of my mound, then she thrust her tongue into my mouth, groaning loudly as I rubbed her wet vulva. I loved the feel of her downy pubic hair against my belly, and as much as I wanted to bury my face in her pussy, there was something sweet and romantic about pressing our bodies together in the missionary style.

As I began rocking my hips back and forth against hers, I felt her hard button flapping against mine while I coated the insides of her thighs with my juices. Brooke dug her fingernails into my back as she pressed her pussy harder against mine with her breathing slowly ratcheting up in intensity.

"Yes, Jade," she grunted. "You feel so good."

"Even better than my vibrator?" I teased.

"Fuck, yes," she panted. "You're warm and soft, and *much more* responsive. *Come* with me, Jade. I'm getting close...."

"*Brooke,*" I panted in her ear, feeling my pleasure rapidly spreading inside me. "I feel so close to you..."

"Uhnn," Brooke groaned, wrapping her legs tightly around my ass. "I'm cumming, Jade! Cum with me!"

Suddenly I felt the floodgates open as my hips began shaking over Brooke's steaming pussy. For the next thirty seconds, we bucked our hips wildly together, holding each other close and kissing each other passionately. My mind was swimming in delirious pleasure, not only because of the intense contractions emanating from between my legs, but because I knew Brooke and I had reached a new level of intimacy. I hadn't felt this close to anyone in a long time, and as we held each other tightly in the pitch dark, Brooke whispered in my ear that she loved me too.

5

———————

rooke and I fell asleep in each other's arms not long after, and when I awoke she was nestled with her back against my tummy. I reached around and caressed her breasts, and she purred softly. Then she turned her face toward me, and I kissed her gently.

"Mmm," she purred. "I could get used to this."

"Me too," I said, wrinkling my forehead as I peered into her eyes. "But I don't know how much longer we'll have a chance to be together like this."

She flipped over to face me and smiled, ignoring the black cloud that seemed poised to burst our bubble.

"We better get *busy* then," she said, rubbing her breasts playfully against mine. "You seem to have more experience with this sort of thing than I do. Teach me how to make love to a woman. I want to learn *everything* about you."

"It's not so different than you might expect," I said, temporarily forgetting my troubles as I nibbled my way down her neck. "Just do what comes naturally. You'll know when you're hitting the right buttons."

Brooke arched her back, lifting her chest to meet my face.

"Yes, Jade," she mewed. "Kiss my body all over. I want to learn how to please you like your other partners."

"*You're* the only partner I want right now," I said, rolling my tongue over her raised areolas, wondering how much sexual experience she'd actually had. "I love your pretty breasts. Have you ever been kissed like this before?"

"Never like *that*," she groaned. "Boys just go straight for my nipples and suck on them like they're inhaling a milkshake."

"The key is to go slow and *worship* a woman's body," I chuckled. "Girls are different from boys in the way they get aroused and experience sexual pleasure. It's not just about sticking it in and getting off. You have to *tease* your partner, build up her excitement, and let her enjoy the journey instead of focusing on the destination."

"Mmm, I like that metaphor," Brooke sighed as I squeezed her breasts while teasing the base of her nipples with little circles of my tongue. "This trip has exceeded my expectations in *so* many ways. I never expected to find my soulmate in the middle of the desert."

I could feel my heart beating faster and faster the more Brooke talked about how she felt about me, but I wasn't sure if it was because I shared similar feelings, or because I knew she'd soon be wrenched away from me. But at this moment, that was the last thing I wanted to think about. I just wanted to revel in her body and bring her to new heights of pleasure.

I pinched her nipples, feeling them harden between my fingers, then I placed my lips over one of her teats and sucked it like a lollypop, swirling my tongue around the edges as Brooke groaned in pleasure.

"*Jade*," she whispered. "I love the way you make love to me. I want to feel you caress *every* part of my body."

I smiled as Brooke's hips began to undulate in expectation against my belly while I kissed my way down the center of her stomach. When I reached her navel, I pressed my tongue inside her cavity and swirled it around the perimeter, foreshadowing what we both knew was soon to come.

"Uhnn," she moaned, lifting her hips off the bed and grinding her wet pussy against my breasts nestled between her thighs. I rocked my tits against her opening, feeling her juices coat me like maple syrup.

I nibbled my way further down her abdomen until I reached her soft muff, rolling my face over her downy fur. As much as I enjoyed a bare pussy, it was always a delight whenever I encountered a full patch of pubic hair, since it reminded me of my partner's innocence. Brooke was still too young and inexperienced to succumb to the societal pressure to trim her bush. I could taste her dewy sweetness on the tips of her hair, and as she rocked her pussy against the front of my neck, I smiled, knowing how much I was turning her on.

"*Lick me*, Jade," she begged. "I want to feel you kissing me the way you did last night."

"Mmm," I purred, lowering my face to her fragrant pussy, licking the sides of her slit while I tasted her honey.

The closer my tongue came to her opening, the wider she spread her knees, pulling my face closer to her snatch. I extended my tongue and pressed it inside her hole, and she groaned, gripping the sheets on either side of her hips.

"Oh God, Jade," she sighed. "Fuck me with your tongue. That feels so good."

I grinned, realizing this was a whole new experience for her, so different from the feeling of the plastic vibrator buzzing inside her yesterday. There was no substitute for a warm body lying next to a woman–licking, sucking, and caressing her body with her soft skin.

I gripped the sides of Brooke's hips with my hands and pulled her closer to me, burying my face in her sopping pussy. She began rocking her vulva faster and faster against my face, and I could tell from the pace of her breathing that she was going to come soon. But I wanted to feel her in my mouth when she came, and I pulled out of her hole and swiped my tongue up towards her apex like I was licking an ice cream cone. When I reached her flaring jewel, she gasped and threw her head back against the pillow.

"*Oh my God!*" she gasped. "This is *so* much better than a vibrator. I had no idea it could be this good."

"You've never been kissed down here before?" I said, peering up at her from under the covers.

"Nothing like this. The few boys I've been with never seem to be able to *find* it, let alone spend time pleasuring me there. They only seem interested in one thing. I had no idea how good this could feel."

"We've hardly just begun, baby," I said, encircling her gland with my lips, rolling my tongue over it gently.

"*Fuckkk*," Brooke hissed, pulling the undersheet up harder toward her. "Suck me, Jade. I want to come in your mouth."

"Mmm," I nodded, too busy teasing her clit to come up for air.

While Brooke slowly titled her hips toward me, I felt her buttock muscles clenching in my palms as I gripped her ass tightly. With her chest rising and falling in erratic gasps, her legs began to quiver, and I buried my nose in her dripping pubic hair as she began to lift her hips off the mattress.

"Jade," she squealed. "I'm going to cum. Oh God, I'm going to cum in your sweet mouth. Feel me Jade! Feel me–"

Suddenly, Brooke grabbed the back of my head and pulled me hard against her pussy while her hips began quaking against my face. I could feel her juices running down over my neck and tits as her pussy began spasming in powerful contractions.

"*Jade, Jade, Jade...*" she panted with each contraction. "I'm cumming. I'm cumming in your beautiful mouth."

Up to this point, I'd hardly paid any attention to my own pleasure while I concentrated on pleasing Brooke. But when I felt her shaking against my face and she began wailing in ecstasy, suddenly my own pussy pulsed in sympathy as I began gushing all over the sheets between my legs. I held her softly in my mouth until she stopped quivering, then I lifted my head and kissed her soft pubic patch, inhaling her heavenly aroma. Then I pulled myself up next to her and kissed her as we intermingled our tongues.

"Oh my God," she said when we finally pulled ourselves apart. "I've never been made love to like that before. That was the most beautiful, erotic, tender thing I've ever experienced."

"I'm glad you liked it baby," I smiled. "I felt exactly the same way. I like making love to you."

"What about *you* now?" she said, propping herself up on an elbow. "I want to learn how to please you the same way. I've been dreaming about licking you down there for two days..."

"There's still plenty of time for that," I said, pinning her back down onto the bed. "But this time I want to *see* you while I make love to you. No more hiding under the covers and rubbing our bodies together in the dark."

"I like the sound of that," Brooke smiled. "But when do *I* get to be on top?"

"Maybe next time," I grinned, placing my ass over her pelvis. "You said you wanted me to teach you how to make love to a woman. Well this time, I'm gonna *fuck* you. Sometimes you want it soft and sometimes you want it hard. This time I want it *hard*."

"Fuck yes," Brooke hissed. "Fuck me, Jade. I want to look into your eyes while you fuck me."

"You're reading my mind, girl," I said. "Now lift up one knee and spread your legs."

"That sounds dirty–"

"Sometimes dirty is *good*," I smiled, straddling her extended leg and lowering my pussy toward her crotch.

When our vulvas touched, Brooke groaned and reached up to squeeze my tits.

"Mmm, yes," she purred. "I'm going to enjoy watching you fuck me. Plus, I get to play with *other* parts of you while we watch each other."

"Exactly," I said, pulling the underside of her raised leg against my stomach as I pressed my cunt hard against hers.

"Uhnn," Brooke whinnied, squeezing my tits tighter. "Your pussy's so wet."

"That's at least half *you*, girl," I grunted, pulling her tighter against me.

As we began to rock our hips together, Brooke reached out her hands to me, and I intertwined my fingers with hers, clasping her hands tightly.

"You're so beautiful," she said, peering at me with a sad expression. "I love watching you make love to me."

"You too, babe," I smiled, happy she was recognizing the distinction. Although I was fucking her in every sense of the word, at this moment, I felt closer to her than I ever had.

"I'm going to come soon, hun," I said, suddenly feeling overwhelmed with the sights and sounds of this sweet angel lying prone underneath me.

"Yes, Jade," Brooke said. "Let me watch you come while we're connected together."

I was surprised how quickly I'd reached the height of my passion, but there was something about the sight of my new lover peering up at me bittersweetly while squeezing my hands that put me over the edge. We both knew that we'd soon have to part company, and the thought of it tore us both apart.

As my body began quivering atop hers, a small tear streamed out of my eye and rolled down my cheek. No words were necessary between us as our bodies began shaking together and we peered into each other's eyes. After we came down from our climaxes, I slumped over onto her body, feeling her soft breath caressing the side of my ear. I didn't know how much longer I'd be with Brooke, but in this moment, I just wanted to hold her forever.

6

———

Brooke and I made love for the rest of the morning, then we got back in the car and headed south along I-25 toward Colorado and the Grand Canyon. As we marveled at the spectacular scenery of the snow-capped Rocky Mountains, neither of us was very talkative knowing we were getting ever-closer to the west coast where we'd have to part company. But after a half hour of pensively looking out her side window, Brooke suddenly laughed.

"What?" I asked.

"I was just thinking back to the incident outside our motel yesterday..."

"What was so funny about that?"

"*Wood chipper?*" she said, looking at me with a raised eyebrow.

"Huh?"

"When you said to that guy that was threatening you that you'd cut him up like a wood chipper if he got any closer."

I chuckled, realizing how ridiculous that sounded after the fact.

"It was the best I could think of in the heat of the moment."

"Well it sure worked," she said. "You scared the crap out of both of those guys."

"Well, good riddance," I said, peering over at Brooke. "Who needs *boys* anyway, right?"

"After last night," she smiled, "I can't imagine I'll ever want to turn back."

I gazed out my windscreen for the next few minutes, thinking about Brooke's future life. Was it really fair of me to steal her affections when she'd be leaving so soon? Was it even fair for me to try to turn her against boys her own age? She had her whole life ahead of her and there'd be so many new and exciting opportunities in California.

"Have you been thinking much about L.A. these past few days?" I said.

"A little bit," she said. "I'm a bit worried, to be honest. Being all alone, competing with all those beautiful people in Hollywood. Do you think I'll be able to make a go of it?"

I reached over the console and squeezed her hand gently.

"Well, since I met you, you've reminded me at different moments of Marilyn Monroe, Elizabeth Taylor, Geena Davis, and Kristen Stewart. I think you can hold your own against *anyone*. I wouldn't be surprised to see you on the big screen one day."

"Opposite *Robert Pattinson* maybe?" she said.

"Is that your leading man type?"

"Well, he *is* kind of dreamy," Brooke said. "Or maybe it was just that whole romantic premise of the Twilight story line."

"So you're saying you dig *vampires*?"

Brooke chuckled softly, then peered back outside her window at the passing landscape. The road was almost devoid of cars as we rolled by the broad ranches of southern Wyoming. Suddenly, a lone figure appeared on the horizon, about a half a mile ahead of us on the side of the road. It appeared to be another hitchhiker. As we got closer, we saw that it was a young man wearing a cowboy hat and faded jeans. Brooke suddenly perked up, squinting through the windshield. When we passed by, we couldn't help noticing how handsome he was.

Brooke turned to look at me with wide eyes.

"Did you *see* that?" she said.

"Uh-huh. He was kind of cute, wasn't he?"

"Cute?" she said. "That was one sexy-ass cowboy."

"Well he's no Brad Pitt. But I suppose he'd do in a pinch."

"Aren't you going to *stop*?" she said, furrowing her brow like a sad puppy dog.

I took my foot off the gas pedal for a moment, considering her request. As much as I wanted to have Brooke for myself the rest of the trip, I knew this would be the perfect opportunity to wean her off me and begin making some new friends with people her own age.

I peered back at her and smiled as I pulled off the road. Then I honked my horn twice and began to back up along the shoulder. I had no idea where the boy was headed or how long he'd stay with us, but something told me the sparks were about to fly once again with my pretty, young wayfarer.

VOLUME FOUR

THE HOUSESITTER

1

As I finished packing my bags for my two-week vacation to Bora Bora, my heart pounded with excitement. I hadn't been away from home for this long in years, and I could already feel the warm sea breeze on my face. Even though it was early March in Chicago, I'd chosen to wear light Bermuda shorts and open sandals so I could enjoy the tropical lifestyle the moment I stepped off the plane. I was ready to leave the melting snow and biting wind-chill of the midwestern winter far behind.

But I was anxious for another reason. I was about to leave the security of my valuable home and the care of my beloved tabby cat in the hands of a teenager I barely knew. I'd seen her grow up over the years as the daughter of my best friend, but this was the first time she'd be responsible for managing an entire household on her own. Granted, her mother lived only a half-hour away, but there was still a lot of mischief a high school senior could get into left to her own devices for so long. I had visions of her holding wild house parties and her friends trashing the place while the neighbors looked on disapprovingly as the cops raided the place.

The only comfort I had was knowing I'd be able to monitor the property 24/7 using my recently installed security system. With five

Wi-Fi-enabled cameras installed at key locations in and around the house, I'd be able to watch and listen for any unusual activity directly from my iPhone. I was a bit concerned about invading my housesitter's privacy, but I'd already informed her of the setup and both she and her mother seemed okay with the arrangement.

Besides, it wasn't as if I'd be spying on her in private areas like the bathroom and bedroom. I just wanted to make sure that the main points of ingress and egress were protected and that high-value areas of my house could be watched. I'd had the system installed for *her* safety as much as my own.

Or so I'd convinced myself.

As I carried my suitcases downstairs, I heard the soft chime of the doorbell. I looked at my watch and saw that I had four hours before my flight departure.

Good girl, I thought. She's already demonstrating responsibility by arriving on time for our scheduled briefing. Even though I'd emailed her intricate instructions, there were still a few important details I wanted to go over.

But when I opened the door, I wasn't quite ready for what I saw. The cute freckle-faced teenager I'd known in her youth had blossomed into a beautiful, curvy, full-figured woman. Wearing tight stretch jeans and a form-fitting sweater, she reminded me of the statuesque actress Christina Hendricks from the TV series Mad Men. I hadn't seen her for quite a few months, and she seemed to have a whole new confidence about her.

"Hi Jenny," I stammered, catching my breath. "Please, come in. Do you need some help with your bags?"

"No thanks, Mrs. Jackson," she smiled, lifting her small suitcase, stepping into my vestibule. She had flushed cheeks from the cold weather outside and she rubbed her hands together to warm them up as I closed the door.

"You must be freezing in those light clothes," I said. "Didn't you bring a jacket?"

"I wasn't planning on leaving the house very much," she said. "I've got lots of homework to keep me busy during the school break."

I nodded my head, knowing she was gearing up for college in the fall.

"Yes, I suppose so," I said. "But at least the garage is heated, and you'll have the full use of my car while I'm away if you need anything. So hopefully you'll have minimal exposure to the elements."

"Thanks," Jenny said. "I'll take good care of your property, I promise."

"It'll be good training for college," I smiled. "Is this the first time you've been on your own for this long?"

"Other than the occasional babysitting gig, yes."

"I've stocked up the fridge and left instructions for everything in the kitchen, so hopefully it won't be too much trouble. Why don't you bring your bags and leave them at the bottom of the stairs while I get you up to speed?"

Jenny followed me down the hall and dropped her bags at the landing to my stairs, then I led her into the kitchen and swung open the pantry door.

"The most important thing is making sure Oscar is properly fed and keeping his litter box clean. I've pulled out two cans of cat food and a bag of kibble and placed them on the kitchen island. All the other instructions are on the fridge door."

Oscar jumped up on top of the island when he heard the familiar rustling of his kibble bag, and Jenny rubbed his shoulders while I continued the briefing.

"I give him two scoops of kibble in his dish by the door in the morning and try to keep his water dish at least half-filled with fresh water at all times. Then another half-can of wet food around six p.m. and a few mouthfuls of kibble whenever he seems needy."

"He seems pretty amenable," Jenny said, listening to him purr as she gently stroked his back.

"He's pretty low maintenance," I nodded, happy to see Oscar warming up to her so fast. "Give him a little bit of cuddling a few times a day and he's pretty happy. Let me show you where I keep his litter box."

I led Jenny to my main-floor laundry room and opened a closet door revealing a large bag of cat litter.

"His litter box is under the laundry sink. If you clean it once every couple of days, it will keep the smell under control. Just scoop up any clumps you see with the little ladle and place it in this covered waste can. If it gets full, the trash collection comes every Tuesday and Friday, but honestly it should be fine for the two weeks you're here. If the litter gets low, refill as necessary using this bag."

I pointed to a cat toy resting atop one of the shelves.

"If you feel like playing with him every now and then to keep him from getting bored, he loves playing this little cat-and-mouse game."

I picked up the toy fishing rod and dangled a stuffed mouse above his head while he playfully batted at it. After I placed the device on the dryer, Jenny picked it up and pulled the mouse along the floor in front of Oscar's face as he chased after it. I couldn't help noticing her round ass in her tight jeans as she wiggled her hips to simulate the mouse scurrying along the floor.

"Perfect," I smiled with a slight flush in my face. "You two will be best friends in no time. Of course, you're welcome to use the washer and dryer at your leisure. The controls are pretty self-explanatory."

"I'm used to doing my own laundry, so no problem," Jenny nodded.

I led her back to the kitchen and placed my keys on the island countertop.

"These are the keys to the house and the car. Instructions for the TV remote are on the table beside my sofa. You're also welcome to use my computer in the office if you need to print anything or do some extra homework. The login password is Oscar123."

I glanced into my backyard and motioned to the pool.

"One other thing. I've uncovered the pool a bit early and turned on the water heater, so if you feel like a refreshing swim or want to use the hot tub, feel free any time."

Jenny looked outside and widened her eyes looking at the rippling turquoise water.

"Wow," she said. "I wasn't expecting that. I'm afraid I didn't bring any swim clothes..."

"I've got some swimsuits in my bedroom dresser upstairs. You're welcome to use those." I glanced at Jenny's large breasts and chuckled. "Though I'm not sure you'll fit into them very comfortably."

"I'll find a way to make do," she smiled.

"Okay then," I said, suddenly aware of the twitch in my pussy. "Everything else is pretty self-explanatory, but if you have any questions or run into any trouble you can text me on my phone. I should have it with me most of the time, but if there's an emergency you can also call my neighbor Betty, whose number is on the fridge."

"I hope you won't be looking at your phone *too* much while you're on vacation," Jenny smiled. "Isn't that the whole point of going on vacation? To get away from all those everyday troubles?"

"Of course," I said, pulling my cell phone out of my purse. "I don't intend to, but I wanted to remind you that I've got cameras set up in various places throughout the house to keep an eye on things. I'll be checking in periodically to make sure you're not having any wild parties or burning the place down."

"Not to worry, Mrs. Jackson," Jenny chuckled. "Between the pool, the TV, and the computer, I've got plenty of other things to keep me amused."

I smiled at her, admiring her voluptuous figure.

"There are no cameras in the private areas like as the bedroom and washrooms, so you don't have to worry about your personal privacy." I pointed outside the kitchen door, where a small wireless camera hung from the eavestrough. "But just so you know, one camera keeps an eye on the backyard, and there's also one at each of the exit doors, and one at the top and bottom of the central stairway, all of which can pan and tilt to provide wide coverage of each area. So you might want to keep your clothes on while you're scampering around the house."

"No problem with the cameras," Jenny smiled. "I'm used to having my parents keeping close tabs on me already."

"I'll bet," I said, trying not to undress her with my eyes. "You must be dying to head off to college in a few months. All those cute boys and toga parties–you'll think you'd died and gone to heaven."

"I'm not really into all that..." Jenny said, shrugging her shoulders.

"Not even *boys*? There'll be a whole new set of rules once you get onto campus."

"We'll see," Jenny said, glancing at my cleavage in my tight cotton blouse. "I'm sure there'll be plenty of other distractions when I get there."

"Um, yes," I said, momentarily taken aback by her sudden change in demeanor. I heard a honk from the driveway and glanced at my watch. "That must be my taxi. Did you have any more questions before I head off for the airport?"

"I think I'm good to go," Jenny said. "Enjoy your trip and don't worry about Oscar or your house. Everything will be just like you left it when you come back."

"Thanks, Jenny," I said, leaning in to give her a peck on the cheek. "Thanks again for looking after things while I'm away. I've transferred four hundred dollars to your account for the initial deposit. I'll pay the second installment when I return."

"Sounds great," Jenny said, cradling a purring Oscar in her arms. "But if everything turns out to be *this* easy, I might have to issue a refund."

"You're going to need every penny you can earn for college," I said. "It's the least I can do."

I carried my bags out to the driveway and the taxi driver placed them in the trunk, then I nestled into the back seat. It wasn't until I sat down that I realized how wet my panties had become. I wasn't sure if it was the feel of Jenny's skin on my lips that had gotten my juices flowing, or her comment about having other distractions at college. Had her glance at my cleavage projected an interest in something other than *boys*?

Either way, something told me that I'd be checking my phone more often than either of us expected while I was on my little South Pacific excursion.

2

By the time I checked in for my flight and cleared through security at the airport, it was already starting to get dark. When I got to the waiting area at my departure gate, I picked up a magazine and tried to distract myself while waiting for the flight to board. But I couldn't stop thinking about Jenny. I was absolutely floored by her transformation from a skinny freckle-faced freshman to a stunning, statuesque high school senior. Not only did she have a figure that made my mouth water, but some of her reactions suggested she was just as interested in me as I was with her.

Did her comment about not being into boys and her frequent glances at my cleavage signal she was attracted to women, like me? And when I mentioned that she might not fit into my bathing suit and she responded by saying that she'd find a way to 'make do', did that mean she was intending to swim in her underwear or–God forbid–in the *buff*?

The more I thought about it, the wetter my panties became as I squirmed uncomfortably in my chair. I glanced up at the display board behind the gate agent's desk and saw that I still had fifteen minutes before the plane began boarding.

What the fuck, I murmured, pulling my phone out of my purse, tapping on the home security app. It won't hurt to check up on her before I depart for the first leg of my flight to Hawaii. If only to make sure Oscar's water bowl is filled.

Yeah, *right*, I smiled, knowing full well that I just wanted to catch another glimpse of her sexy body.

When the app opened, it showed two side-by-side panes displaying the camera locations inside the house. Seeing no sign of Jenny in either picture, I tapped on each one and toggled my finger across the screen to angle the camera to pan the upstairs and down-stairs living areas.

Okay, I said, tilting my head. *Maybe she's in the bedroom or the bathroom getting ready to turn in.*

I waited a few minutes, but still seeing no sign of activity, I swiped my thumb to the left to view the two cameras covering the outside doors. She wouldn't have any reason to be outside in the cold weather, unless she'd stepped outside to have a smoke. But she didn't strike me as the type. Shaking my head in dismay, I swiped to the last two images displaying views of the backyard and the garage.

Still no sign of Jenny.

What the hell, I cursed. Where is she hiding? She couldn't have taken off so soon after I'd left. The car was still parked in the garage, so I knew she hadn't gone out for more provisions.

I was just about to tap the playback feature on the inside cameras to track her previous movement when I noticed a shadowy figure moving around the pool image. A curvy girl wearing a terry-cloth robe walked toward the shallow end of the basin, then dropped her robe on the patio and stepped into the steaming water.

"Holy shit!" I exclaimed, recognizing her hourglass figure and her long, corkscrew hair. *She's naked! And she's going to skinny dip in my pool!*

The outdoor security camera had detected her movement and turned on the security lamp, illuminating her body like a pale appari-tion against the reflecting surface of the pool. Covering her breasts with crossed arms over her chest, she slowly lowered herself into the water then began doing gentle breast strokes across the thirty-foot-long pit.

As I watched her silvery body gliding through the water like a translucent nymph, I suddenly became aware of the moisture building up between my legs. Even though I could only see the back of her body partially obscured by the swirling water, I could clearly make out the cleft in her ass and the exquisite curvature of her hips as she flapped her legs in and out in a gentle whipping motion.

Jesus Christ, I panted, imagining she was scissoring her legs against something *else* right now.

When she reached the end of the pool and turned around to swim the opposite length, I could see her pretty face illuminated by the bright spotlight as her head bobbed up and down in the shimmering water.

Oh my God, I muttered under my breath, scarcely believing what I was seeing.

I began to spread my legs unconsciously, imagining her burying her face in my pussy as I watched her beautiful ass rising and falling in the tumbling surf. I placed two fingers on the screen and pinched them together, zooming in on her figure slicing through the water. As she swam back and forth across the pool, I traced her motion by drawing my finger slowly across the screen to turn the camera in lock-step with her movement.

I was so mesmerized by the intoxicating scene on my phone, I barely heard the announcement over the public address system for the last call to board my plane. I looked up, and noticing the diminishing line of passengers streaming onto the jet bridge, I picked up my bags and scurried to the end of the queue.

Fuck! I cursed under my breath, trying to balance my iPhone in my hand while I fumbled with my boarding pass.

I just prayed that I'd be able to access the airport's Wi-Fi signal from inside the plane so I wouldn't have to miss another second of watching her sexy figure.

When I nestled into my seat by the window, I turned my body away from my seatmates and pulled my phone close to my breast so I could watch her without any further interruption. The last thing I needed was for someone to catch me leering at her like I was watching some kind of porn video. But just as Jenny paused by the pool-side ladder preparing to lift herself out of the water, the flight attendant announced over the p.a. system that we had to turn off our electronic devices in preparation for take-off.

You've got to be kidding me, I cursed as I watched Jenny reach up onto the handles.

"Madam?" a flight attendant said, leaning over the aisle. "Please turn off your phone and connect your seat belt. We're about to take off."

I peered up at her with my mouth agape, as if supplicating divine intervention. The timing couldn't have been worse. Just as I tapped the power button on the side of my phone, I saw the top of Jenny's dripping breasts rise out of the pool before the screen faded to black. Gritting my teeth in frustration, I checked the information folder in the back pocket of the seat in front of me to learn how to connect to the airplane's inflight Wi-Fi network. I didn't want to miss one more unnecessary second of spying on this sexy vixen if I could avoid it. Even if she'd gotten dressed by the time I got back online, I could still use the replay button to watch the entire scene from start to finish over and over.

Thank God for modern technology, I said to myself, noticing a large wet spot had formed in the front of my shorts.

Forty-five agonizing minutes later, after the plane had reached cruising altitude, I heard a chime and looked up to see that the seat belt sign had been turned off. It was now okay to power back up my electronic devices. I pressed the power button on my phone, tapping my foot impatiently while I waited for the home screen to light up.

When I saw the familiar apps appear on the screen, I tapped the settings icon then clicked the Wi-Fi function to join the air carrier's proprietary inflight service. They were charging an outrageous $24.99 for a full-flight pass, but at this point I would have paid ten times that amount to get back online. After entering my credit card information and agreeing to the terms, I saw the three delta-shaped bars alight on the top left-hand side of my phone screen.

Okay, we're back in business, I huffed, clicking the home security app until it opened up to the pool-cam view. But when the image appeared, there was no longer any sign of Jenny anywhere in the backyard.

Of course she would have gone back indoors after coming out of the pool, I said to myself. *It's freezing cold at this time of the day in Chicago!*

I was about to tap the replay button so I could watch her naked body slicing through the water again when my finger paused over the glass.

Unless...

Could she have jumped in the hot tub to relax and stay warm after her late evening swim? Could I be that lucky?

I swiped my thumb down to tilt the camera closer to the front of the house, and my heart skipped a beat when I saw Jenny submerged in the churning water with her arms outstretched over the rim. Her body was turned away from the neighbors' yards, directly facing the camera. The top of her tits poked out of the swirling water like two pink balloons, dancing atop the churning eddy.

She had a quiet, blissful look on her face, but I could see her body shifting under the opaque surface of the water. For a moment, I thought it was just the action of the powerful jets pushing against her body from all directions. But there was something about the way she was moving her shoulders and adjusting her position on the seat that led me to believe there was something more going on.

Could she possibly be...?

I knew from plenty of personal experience just how pleasurable it was to position the jets directly in front of my pussy. With the powerful rush of water flowing over my clit, there was nothing quite so heavenly as the feel of the warm water caressing my most sensitive part. When Jenny lowered her hands under the water and angled her arms toward her crotch, there was no longer any doubt.

She was playing with herself under the water!

As I watched her lean her head back against the top of the hot tub and her mouth begin to part open, I suddenly felt a rush of heat and wetness to my own aching pussy.

She certainly didn't waste any time making herself comfortable in my house, I smiled.

But I could tell from her position in the tub that she was missing the ideal placement to receive the most direct stimulation.

Move two feet to your left! I wanted to shout at her while I stared at my phone screen. *There's a jet perfectly positioned to stimulate your clit! You haven't lived until you've come from one of those things!*

I remembered that I'd added a two-way audio feature to each of the cams so I could send a warning message to any potential burglars caught by my motion sensors. For a brief moment, I considered turning it on to encourage her to take full advantage of the hot tub's special features. But this was no *burglar*–this was my young housesitter who must have thought I was far out of earshot by now flying over the Pacific Ocean.

Besides, even if I could reach out to her this way, how could I possibly hope to carry on such an intimate conversation without attracting the suspicion of my fellow passengers sitting only inches away?

But it didn't take long for Jenny to figure it out. Her arms stretched out to her sides as she searching for the precise location of each of the water nozzles. When she leaned forward a few inches and felt the jet shooting up from the edge of the bench a few seats over, she froze for a moment as her eyes widened in excitement. It only took a few seconds for her to move directly over the pulsating stream as she slumped her body lower into the water.

Suddenly, her mouth gaped open as she felt the powerful jet pulsing against her sensitive nub. I knew immediately what she was feeling, and I ached to be lying next to her, feeling her body shaking as she reveled in the rising pleasure administered by the powerful spray. She tilted her head further back against the rim, then her elbows flared out from her sides as she squeezed her tits under the swirling water.

Fuck me, I cursed, wishing it were *my* hands caressing her gorgeous melons instead of her own. I dreamed how I'd ravage her in the sensuous whirlpool while hidden from the prying eyes of my neighbors under the cloak of the swirling water.

I sat captivated as Jenny's mouth gaped progressively wider from the intense pleasure building inside her. When her climax finally washed over her, her head began jerking back and forth while her face scrunched up into the most exquisite form of ecstasy. I almost came along with her, squeezing my thighs tightly together trying to keep my body from writhing in sympathy with her next to my oblivious seat mates.

After she stopped trembling in the swirling water, Jenny lay back against the seat of the hot tub and slumped her shoulders in delirious exhaustion. She had the cutest flush on her face, and for a brief moment, I thought she glanced up at the security camera perched only a few feet away from the tub.

Had she suspected that I was watching her the whole time? Did she notice the movement of the camera as I traced her movement in the pool and the hot tub? Or heard the soft whirring of the camera as I zoomed in on her face when she came?

If so, what was already the most stimulating thing I'd witnessed in a long time, suddenly became even more arousing. I needed to release my pent-up sexual tension, and fast. I peered over at the lavatory sign nearest me and noticed that it was vacant. I waited a few minutes until Jenny stepped out of the hot tub, revealing her glorious glistening body, before I asked to be excused.

The moment I locked the lavatory door behind me, I tore off my clothes and thrust three fingers deep inside my sopping pussy, fucking myself furiously. It must have taken less than ten seconds for me to pop off with the most powerful orgasm I'd had in months. As I stood quivering over the sink with my hand embedded in my snatch, I looked up at the mirror and smiled.

I suddenly knew that I wouldn't be so alone on this trip after all.

3

———

When I returned to my seat, I switched over to the indoor cams and noticed that Jenny had gone upstairs, flitting back and forth between the master bedroom and bath. She'd changed into flannel pajamas with a Little Mermaid pattern, and I smiled at the contrast of the girly cartoon images with her sexy, curvy figure. The upstairs camera was installed at the top of the stairs, but she'd left the bedroom door ajar just enough for me to angle the camera to see the edge of the bed.

When she emerged from the bathroom, she picked up a book from the nightstand and propped up the pillows to provide a comfortable reading position. Then she sat down on the bed and began reading with her legs crossed over one another. As she wiggled her bare toes while she read, I zoomed in the camera to examine her face more closely.

Her auburn hair fell softly against her pale cheeks in gentle ringlets, highlighting her speckled cheekbones. She had large eyes with brilliant green irises, framed by dark eyebrows arching seductively over long lashes. And her slender nose had a slight upturn at the end, accentuating her puffy rosebud lips and cleft chin. Wearing virtually no makeup, she looked like a fashion doll from a Bergdorf Goodman department store.

The perfect model of young, sensual beauty, I thought.

While she read her book, her gaze stayed focused just below the line of sight of the camera down the hall. As much as I wanted to zoom out to take in more of her breathtaking body, I was afraid the noise might attract her attention and she'd catch me spying on her again. But after a while, she placed the book beside her on the bed and peered around my bedroom, looking for another distraction.

Much to my horror, she leaned over and pulled open the drawer to my bedside night stand. The noise of the drawer gave me an opportunity to zoom back out, and I saw her eyes widen as she peered inside at the contents. I'd thought about hiding my sex toys in another location, but I hadn't imagined she'd be bold enough to go fishing around in my personal effects.

Cheeky girl, I smiled, noticing my breathing rate becoming more raspy.

I kept a whole treasure trove of toys next to the bed, and it must have looked like a veritable candy store to a young teenager just turning the corner into adulthood. She pulled out each device one at a time, examining it closely before placing it on the side of the bed beside her.

The first one was the long and sturdy Magic Wand, my trusty industrial-strength vibrator that delivered a powerful and sustained jolt directly to the clitoris. She held the handle vertically in her left hand and gripped the flexible ball at the top, bending it forward and back with her other hand. Then she pulled out my tiny Pocket Rocket and twisted the end, feeling the nubby head beginning to buzz softly in her hand. When she reached in and removed the salami-sized, two-sided silicone dildo that I used whenever I had a special friend over, I grimaced in embarrassment. She grasped the double-headed penis at each end and bent it forward and back into a U-shape, pinching her eyebrows and shaking her head in dismay.

It must have been a shock to her young sensibilities to discover all the naughty ways a woman could stimulate herself with the wide assortment of sex aids on the market. Or maybe she was just trying to fathom how the demure Mrs. Jackson, who she'd known since childhood, had become such a perverted sex addict.

Not so demure now, am I little girl? I smiled, feeling my juices beginning to flow again in my tight Bermuda shorts.

She reached back into the drawer and pulled out a strange-looking device that looked like a balled fist with two fingers pointing up in a V-shape. Jenny held up my familiar JimmyJane vibrator and inserted her finger between the two appendages. Then she tapped the button on the base and smiled as the little digits fluttered against her hand.

Mmm, yes, I nodded toward the screen. *It feels even better when you place your clit between the vibrating fingers.*

I was getting increasingly worked up watching my young housesitter play with each of the devices, wondering when she was going to try them in the manner they were intended.

She placed the JimmyJane vibrator down on the mattress, then removed a U-shaped object from the drawer and looked at it with a wrinkled brow. She grasped the two ends of the We-Vibe toy and gently flexed it open a few inches. Then she began tapping the buttons on the outside of the device to feel the different vibration settings on each side.

Did she even know which end to put inside? I wondered. She didn't look like she'd had much experience using vibrators. For all I knew, she'd only seen those hard plastic phallic-shaped dildos still prominently displayed in most sex shop windows.

At least she's got a full two weeks to experiment with them, I smiled.

Knowing the best was yet to come, I saw her lean over and extract one of my favorite sex toys, the Rabbit. Shaped like an oversize erect penis, it had a transparent shaft with circulating beads and a protruding thumb-shaped arm with two soft silicone rabbit ears that fluttered against the clitoris. Jenny picked it up and tapped each of the control buttons on the base, watching with amazement as the head of the dildo wobbled like a spinning top while the chrome beads rotated in the middle of the shaft and the rabbit ears fluttered softly against her palm.

Yeah, girl, I smiled. *That one will put you over the top in no time.*

I was intrigued why Jenny hadn't started to experiment with any of the toys by removing her clothes, but I was thrilled that she was showing so much interest in my special collection.

She turned her head toward the open drawer and pinched her eyebrows, peering at the last item in the drawer. When she pulled it out, I smiled, recognizing the distinctive shape of the Ose vibrator. Shaped like a giant flexed finger with a flat base harboring a mysterious hole, she must have wondered how in God's name it worked. But as she began tapping the buttons on the base of the unit, her eyes widened as she watched the long finger begin to flex in a come-hither motion.

But it wasn't until she pressed the button controlling the *lower* part that her eyes really opened in shock and amazement. As it began to pulse in her hand, she drew it closer and squinted at the little hole, watching it pucker in and out like some kind of animatronic mouth. Which is exactly what it was designed to simulate. This was one of my favorite vibrators for exactly that reason, and for a moment I was disappointed that I hadn't packed it for my trip.

But when I saw Jenny pull down her pajama bottoms and spread her knees apart, I quickly forgot about my own needs as I zoomed in to inspect her sex. I gasped when I saw that she'd shaved herself entirely bare, and my pussy spasmed when I saw her glistening pink folds framing her pretty flower.

When she picked up the Ose vibrator and pointed the finger toward her hole, I shifted uncomfortably in my narrow airplane seat, dying to rip off my clothes and spread my legs far apart while I fucked myself watching her. When she inserted the wand into her slit, I groaned audibly, and the woman sitting next to me turned her head, momentarily distracted from the book she was reading.

But when Jenny thrust the device deep into her pussy and tapped the buttons to activate the two human-like functions, I sat up and cleared my throat, trying to keep myself composed. But the rivers of lubrication running down the inside of my thighs made it clear I was anything but composed. I pulled a magazine out of the seat flap in front of me and placed it on my lap to conceal the rapidly darkening wet spot in the crotch of my shorts, turning the phone screen even further away from the prying eyes of the passengers around me. Even though I'd be absolutely mortified if anyone caught me watching the video, there was no way in hell I could stop now, even if the air marshal tried to force me to put it away. They'd have to send in a virtual *army* to wrench this live feed out of my hands.

With the Ose vibrator now pulsing at full speed against Jenny's pussy, she pulled her knees up closer toward her chest and spread her legs further apart. The sight of the fluttering object planted between her legs as she threw her head back against the pillows was driving me insane with desire. But when she unbuttoned the top of her pajamas and began twisting the teats on her voluptuous tits, I couldn't take it anymore.

I excused myself once again, saying I had an upset stomach, and headed back to the lavatory with my phone in hand. As I waited impatiently for the occupant to come out, I inserted my earbuds into the port on the bottom of my phone and tapped the screen to engage the audio function. I could hear Jenny moaning into my ear, and I flapped my legs impatiently, desperately wanting to get into the private room where I could relieve myself.

When the passenger finally opened the door and began to step out, I practically ran him over squeezing into the chamber, slamming the door shut. I placed the phone on top of the sink and pulled my shorts down to my ankles and thrust two fingers into my snatch, pulling the base of my hand hard up against my throbbing clit. As I watched Jenny's knees beginning to flutter with increasing urgency and a deep flush begin to spread over the top of her bosom, I couldn't hold it any longer. As my orgasm washed over me like a tidal wave, I gushed all over my hand and fingers, shaking like I was having an epileptic seizure.

Soon after, Jenny's body also began to convulse as she groaned in the throes of her own powerful climax. As I watched her firm melons bouncing on her chest and her face flush a deep shade of crimson, I moaned along with her until we were both completely spent and exhausted. Then I peered down at my dripping thighs and drenched shorts lying on the floor, wondering how I'd ever be able to return to my seat in such a messy condition. There was no way I could wear these same shorts drenched in my lubrication and God knows how many other people's dried urine from the lavatory floor. There was only one way out of here.

Opening the door a crack, I waited until a female flight attendant passed by, then I quietly called out to her. She turned toward me with a puzzled look and came closer to my door.

"I'm so sorry to bother you about this," I said. "But I've had a bit of an accident and I'm afraid I won't be able to wear these shorts again for the rest of the flight."

She widened her eyes and nodded knowingly. Apparently, I wasn't the only passenger who'd run into this predicament before.

"Can I ask you a huge favor?" I said. "Could you retrieve my carry-on bag from the overhead storage compartment above seat 15F? It's tan colored and has a name tag for J. Jackson."

"No worries, Mrs. Jackson," she said. "I'll be back with your bag in just a moment."

When she returned with my case, I placed it on top of the small vanity and wiped down my legs with a moist towelette. Then I stepped out of my soiled shorts and threw them in the waste receptacle.

I won't be needing those anymore, I murmured to myself. The hard part would be keeping my dick in my pants for the *rest* of the flight to Hawaii. I knew that I'd have to find another distraction to keep me busy so I didn't soil another pair of shorts.

No more Jenny videos until I get to my own private room, I said.

But my mind was already swimming with all the new entertainment possibilities over the course of the next two weeks.

Who needs tropical beaches and chilled mai tai's when you've got the most beautiful, sexy lingerie model at your beck and call whenever you need her?

4

After changing into fresh clothes, I returned to my seat by the window. Even though I was dying to see what Jenny would do next, I dared not reopen the camera app for fear of making another mess. For the rest of the flight to Hawaii, I kept myself distracted watching a movie. A very tame, family-oriented movie. I didn't want to risk viewing another sexy scene that might rekindle my new obsession with my young housesitter.

When we landed in Hawaii, I had to change planes for the next leg of my flight to Bora Bora, so there wasn't any time to check the home security monitors during the brief stopover. By the time I boarded the aircraft, I was so exhausted, I slept the rest of the way to my final destination. When I landed in the archipelago, I took a taxi to my hotel, where a porter escorted me to an overwater bungalow overlooking a turquoise lagoon. I hadn't eaten for eight hours, so I unpacked my bags then headed to the dining room for a sumptuous seafood dinner.

By the time I returned to my room half-intoxicated on margaritas, I was ready to power up my phone and resume watching my new favorite playmate. But with the five-hour time difference between Bora Bora and Chicago, Jenny was already fast asleep, nestled under the warm covers of my bed. It hardly mattered though, since by now I had almost a full day's worth of video to play back any time I wanted.

I tapped the home monitoring app on my phone and toggled back to the upstairs view. I'd left the camera pointed in the direction of the bedroom, so I hoped there'd be plenty more footage of Jenny amusing herself with my toys. But I was disappointed to see that after coming so hard using the Ose vibrator, she'd put the rest of the instruments away before turning in.

I guess after having two powerful back-to-back orgasms, she needed a rest, I smiled. Or maybe she was just pacing herself, leaving room to enjoy the other devices another day.

I came three more times replaying the erotic scenes from the hot tub and my bedroom, over and over. When I finally satiated my lust, I took a relaxing dip in my room's private plunge pool, watching the sun set over the quiet lagoon.

I could get used to this, I thought, taking in the blissful scene.

The only thing missing was a partner to enjoy it with. Maybe I'd bring Jenny back with me next time. The only problem was her mother, who just happened to be my best friend. I didn't want to risk damaging our longstanding relationship. Even if Jenny *had* recently turned eighteen and could make her own decisions.

I fell asleep that night feeling the warm ocean breeze wafting through my veranda window, dreaming of Jenny's naked body gliding through the coral waters of my lagoon. When I woke up, it was already past noon Chicago time, and I flipped over my phone to see what she was up to. I found her sitting at the kitchen island with some school books propped open, making notes in her journal.

Good girl. You don't want to waste your entire spring break playing around the house. You'll need good marks to get into your choice of college in the fall. There'll be plenty of other distractions to keep you amused when you get there.

I walked down to the breakfast bar in the hotel and helped myself to a large serving of eggs Benedict with a side of fresh pineapple and lox. I almost felt sorry leaving Jenny with a fridge full of microwave dinners and pre-cooked casseroles. But something told me she'd find *other* ways to keep herself satisfied while I was away.

I needed to find something to keep my mind off what was happening back home, so I signed up for a snorkeling expedition to a nearby reef. When we arrived there, I marveled at the variety of colorful sea creatures, from striped angelfish to iridescent snapper and giant speckled grouper. I loved swimming among the docile nurse sharks and stingrays, even hitching a brief ride on a large sea turtle. After returning to my room and noticing that I was already a bit sunburned, I pulled off my wet bathing suit and propped myself up in my bed.

When I checked in on Jenny, at first I couldn't see any sign of her in the main rooms of the house or in the backyard. It took a few minutes of angling the upstairs and downstairs cams before I saw her seated in my office, quietly tapping on my keyboard. Although the door was slightly ajar, the line of sight from the ceiling-mounted camera to the office only allowed me to see half of her body.

I remembered leaving my login code if she needed to print anything, but the audio feed didn't indicate any sign of activity other than soft tapping on the keyboard. I hesitated for a moment, thinking I'd give her some peace and quiet and check back later in the evening. Maybe I'd catch her using another one of my sex toys when it was closer to bedtime.

But then I remembered I had *another* app on my phone that provided direct access to my home computer. It was useful when I needed to access important files remotely, but I hadn't used it for a long time. I clicked on the app, and it opened showing my live screen with Jenny's cursor hovering near the top of the web browser. She clicked on the bookmarks tab and began scrolling through my list of saved web addresses.

Forgetting that I'd arranged everything into themed folders, I was mortified when she clicked on the folder for my favorite lesbian porn videos. I used these whenever I felt particularly horny and needed a distraction, but I never intended for anyone *else* to find my private stash. She double-clicked on a link labeled *hot tribbing*, and a window opened showing two naked girls scissoring on an oversize bed. Jenny tapped on the speaker icon at the bottom of the screen and slid the volume bar to the right, and I heard soft moaning wafting out into the hall.

Unsure if it was Jenny's voice or the sounds of the girls on the video, I toggled back to the camera monitoring app. Jenny's left leg was spread far apart with her jeans pulled down to her ankles as she rolled her hips sensuously on the chair. Unable to see what she was doing from the rear position of the camera and with her back turned away from me, I cursed at my inability to watch her more closely. Desperately wanting to see what she was doing while she watched the video, I scanned the remote access menu and noticed a camera icon.

When I clicked the button, my iPhone screen divided into a split window with the tribbing video on one side and Jenny's face on the other. I could only see the top half of her body from the fixed position of the webcam atop my laptop, but that was more than enough. Her cheeks were flushed as she squeezed one of her breasts with her right hand and extended her other arm between her legs in a rhythmic motion.

Holy fuck! I groaned. She was playing with herself while watching a lesbian porn video!

There was no longer any doubt in my mind that she was sexually attracted to women. As I watched her face twist into increasing contortions of pleasure, my eyes darted back and forth between the scene playing out on the porn video and the expression on her face. As the girls on the video began rubbing their pussies together more vigorously, I suddenly heard a familiar buzzing sound coming from the background.

Was she fucking herself with one of my vibrators while she watched the video?

I switched back to the security camera view, but all I could see was Jenny's left leg shaking while her free arm pumped something between her legs. Suddenly overcome with desire, I rushed over to my suitcase and pulled out the one vibrator I'd had the foresight to pack for the trip–my trusty Lelo G-spot stimulator. I thrust the gently curved rod into my snatch and turned the vibration setting up high as I flipped back to the screen monitoring app.

I could hear Jenny moaning along with the two girls on the video as her oversize melons began to tremble from the rising pleasure emanating within her. When the girls suddenly locked their hips, pulling each other tightly toward one another screaming in unison, Jenny's mouth gaped apart, and she uttered a deep guttural groan. With her body jerking forward and back in rhythmic contractions, I grabbed my long dildo with two hands and clamped down on it as I came hard along with Jenny.

It must have taken a full minute for both of us to stop spasming and cumming from the erotic scene we'd both witnessed. I smiled at the irony of getting off watching Jenny while she watched the girls on the video. My mind reeled with all the possibilities for engagement between the two of us when I returned home. Suddenly I realized Jenny was no longer just an innocent high school student, but a fully developed woman, ready to experiment with all the different ways of satisfying her sexual curiosity.

Fortunately for me, Jenny was far from finished quenching her desire for the evening. I saw her right hand move back to the cursor, and she tapped on the progress bar to return to the middle of the video. As it began replaying, she slid the slider slowly to the right until it reached the part where the two girls began pulling their bodies together in preparation for their mutual orgasm.

Jenny peered down, and I heard a deeper kind of throbbing sound emanating from between her legs. As the girls in the video began moaning more loudly, she moved both of her hands between her legs, pounding her pussy with hard jerking motions. I couldn't be sure which vibrator she was using, but the sight of her fucking herself while watching the two girls soon had me thrusting my Lelo vibrator back inside my own pussy. As the girls moved closer to their moment of climax, Jenny's face scrunched up into a painful grimace.

She seemed to be waiting for them to cum once again before she opened the taps. When they finally did, her orgasm was even stronger as she wailed in unison with the girls, jerking her arms forcefully against her body and her compressed tits as she quivered in the office chair. I screamed along with her, feeling my juices spraying out the sides of my pulsating pussy all over my wet thighs and ass.

After Jenny recovered from her second powerful orgasm, she closed the porn site and flipped the laptop cover closed. No longer being able to see her directly, I switched over to the hall cam view, watching her pull up her jeans as she raised herself from the chair. Then she turned around and exited the office, walking toward the stairs. In her right hand, I could see the familiar outline of my purple Rabbit vibrator with its distinctive protruding ears.

I smiled as I watched her head back upstairs to return the vibrator to my nightstand.

That's it, baby, I said. *Take your time trying out each of my special toys. Neither of us is going anywhere for the next two weeks.*

5

———

J enny went to sleep soon after watching the lesbian video, and I decided to go for a relaxing swim in the lagoon to wind down. Between the day's snorkeling activity, a little too much sun, and multiple orgasms watching Jenny on constant replay, I slept like a baby that night. When I woke the following morning, she was back at the kitchen table doing her homework, so I went for another long breakfast at the hotel restaurant.

Since Jenny seemed to be preoccupied with her studies, I decided to make the best use of my time by taking a sailing tour of the island. Wearing a long-sleeved linen shirt, capri pants, and plenty of sunscreen, I wasn't taking any chances at getting more sunburned. With Jenny becoming increasingly bold with her sexual escapades back home, I wanted to make sure I could enjoy watching her without any distractions.

I was surprised how large the island was, taking us more than six hours to circumnavigate the atoll in our sleek, forty-foot catamaran. Formed by an extinct volcano, lush green hillsides rose steeply above the water to over two thousand feet above sea level. I marveled at how clear the water was as I gazed at the endless variety of colorful fish through the sturdy nets joining the two hulls. But by the time we'd finished our mid-day picnic on a secluded beach, I was ready to get out of the sun and back to the relative tranquility of my private cabin.

When the sailboat returned to the hotel, it was already early evening Chicago time, and I was eager to see what mischief Jenny had gotten into while I was away. After I got back to my bungalow, I turned on my phone and saw her taking a swim in the backyard pool wearing a skimpy cream-colored bikini. Looking like a young Ursula Andress from the famous beach scene in the James Bond movie *Dr. No*, she looked even *more* mouth-watering partially covered up.

But this time she wasn't alone. She'd invited a young friend over, and as the two girls splashed each other's faces in the pool, my pussy twitched at the sight of the two scantily clad teens. When they got out of the pool, they moved over to the hot tub, where Jenny encouraged her friend to try out the special seat she'd used the previous day. I could see the look of surprise on her girlfriend's face when she felt the gush of the underwater jet flowing between her legs, but she didn't seem interested in staying there long enough to get properly aroused.

Whether she felt self-conscious stimulating herself in front of her girlfriend or Jenny had warned her that I could be monitoring the property, I wasn't sure. But either way, I enjoyed watching the girls' pretty faces as the swirling water flowed over the tops of their bikini-clad bodies. Just to be safe, I kept the camera zoomed out and the audio turned off for fear of signaling that I was watching them. But they seemed to be enjoying themselves, chatting and giggling as they sipped what looked like two wine coolers.

Thank you, Jenny's girlfriend, I said, *for bringing the alcohol and Jenny's swimsuit*. I hoped it would be just the right combination for loosening the two girls up and taking this spring break adventure to the next level.

After twenty minutes or so of lounging in the tub, the two girls scurried out of the tank and dried themselves off in the kitchen, then headed upstairs to get changed. I followed their movement with the inside cameras, and when they got to my bedroom, I turned on the upstairs audio feed so I could hear what they were saying.

Jenny peeled off her swimsuit then flipped open my nightstand drawer and pointed inside.

"Guess what I discovered last night while I was in Mrs. Jackson's bed?" she said.

Jenny's friend peered into the drawer, then looked up at Jenny with wide eyes.

"Holy shit!" she said. "Are those what I think they are?"

"I can assure you they absolutely are," Jenny smiled.

"But they all look so *different*," her friend said. "I've only seen those gross penis-shaped vibrators. How do these things even *work*?"

Jenny peeled off her swimsuit and jumped on the bed, patting the mattress beside her.

"Why don't you come join me and find out? Some of these devices are really incredible. Don't tell me you've never tried one before."

"Nothing like *that*, that's for sure," her friend said, hesitating.

Jenny reached into the drawer and pulled out the tiny Pocket Rocket vibrator.

"Come on, Niki," she said. "It's just us girls. No one's ever going to know if we have a little extra fun on our sleepover."

"What if Mrs. Jackson's watching on her home security cam?"

Jenny peered down the hallway toward my camera at the top of the stairs, and I quickly turned it so it was facing the other way.

"There's only one camera on each floor, and it can't see in here anyway," Jenny said. "Take your swimsuit off and join me on the bed. We deserve a little break from all our studying."

I heard the sound of clothes dropping to the floor followed by a bed squeaking as her friend joined her on the bed. Then I slowly swiped my finger across the screen, turning the camera back in their direction. Niki was more petite than Jenny, with a typically slender high-school figure. She looked to be about average height and build, but with firm, perky breasts and athletic, toned legs. She sat leaning back against the headboard, with her arms crossed over her chest and her legs extended close together in front of her.

Jenny twisted the base of the Pocket Rocket then handed it to her friend, who ran her fingers over the buzzing end.

"Pretty cool, right?" Jenny said, smiling at Niki, glancing between her legs. "Don't be so bashful. Give it a try."

Niki angled her knees slightly apart and placed the nubby end of the vibrator at the top of her slit, then she suddenly jumped.

"I *know*, right?" Jenny said. "That little thing packs quite a punch, doesn't it?"

"Mmm," Niki nodded, spreading her legs a little further apart.

"You can adjust the intensity of the vibrations by turning the cap on the base of the unit. "I like to ramp it up the more turned on I get."

"How many of these things have you *tried* so far?" Niki said, squirming her hips on the mattress.

"Almost all of them. This is nothing compared to some of the *dual-purpose* vibrators."

"Dual purpose?" Niki said, pinching her eyebrows.

"Most of the other ones stimulate you on the inside and the outside at the same time. You haven't experienced a proper orgasm until you've tried one of these things."

"Why did you give me this *little* one to start with then?" Niki panted, obviously beginning to feel the effects of the targeted stimulation on her clit.

"I didn't want to scare you away too fast," Jenny smiled. "Are you ready to step it up?"

"Definitely," Niki grunted.

"Reach in and take out that pink one that looks like a curled-up snake. I think you're going to like the way it moves inside you."

Niki peered into the drawer and shook her head.

"There's two pink objects that look kind of similar," she said. "Which one?"

"Both," Jenny smiled. "We *both* might be able to get in on the action with this one."

Niki pulled the two objects out of the drawer then Jenny took the smaller piece out of her hand.

"What exactly am I supposed to do with this thing?" Niki said, examining the U-shaped We-Vibe device.

"You slide the fat end inside you with the thinner end pointing up. Then press it all the way up until the connecting part is resting against your opening."

"What are you going to do with the *other* attachment?" Niki said.

"You'll see," Jenny said, flashing her a devilish smile.

Up to this point, I'd just been following the playful banter of the two friends as they tried out the tamer device. But when Niki spread her legs further apart and inserted the thick end of the We-Vibe into her slit, I tore off my pants and reached over for my Lelo vibrator resting on the nightstand. Then I watched Niki press the device deep into her hole until the narrower end rested near the base of her mound.

"This feels kind of weird," Niki said, shaking her head. "How do I turn it on?"

"Leave that up to *me*," Jenny smirked, grasping the remote-control unit and tapping one of the buttons.

"You mean you can–*oh!*" Niki grunted, feeling the internal arm of the We-Vibe unit pulsing against the inside of her pussy.

"Damn straight, girl," Jenny said. "I *told* you Mrs. Jackson has an interesting collection of toys. Let me take the driver's seat while you sit back and enjoy the scenery."

"Mmm," Niki purred, glancing at Jenny's voluptuous tits. "You know I've always fantasized about being with you this way. You have the most amazing body..."

Jenny suddenly leaned over and placed her mouth over one of Niki's tits, sucking her pink teats.

"Oh God, Jenny," Niki panted. "That feels so good..."

"You have *no* idea," Jenny said, flicking her finger over the control knob, activating the clitoral stimulator.

"*Uhnn*," Niki grunted, rolling her hips on the bed as Jenny nibbled her tits and neck. "Fuck me Jenny. Make me come with your hot tongue."

"All in due course, baby," Jenny purred. "I just want you to enjoy this little toy a little longer until you warmed up."

"Oh, I'm getting *warmed up*, alright," Niki groaned, running her fingers through Jenny's hair. "I'm going to cum soon if you keep that up."

"You mean *this*?" Jenny said, flipping the control switch, raising the intensity of the two vibrating arms.

"*Yes!*" Niki panted, thrashing her hips as Jenny suckled on her nubs.

"Oh my God," Niki hissed. "I'm going to come, Jenny. Suck my tits while I cum!"

Suddenly, Niki grabbed the back of Jenny's head with two hands, pulling her face hard against her chest, spreading her legs as far apart as they could go. I zoomed in, watching the vibrator buzzing against her pussy as she slowly lifted her hips off the bed.

"Uhnn!" she groaned, as her orgasm took over her body. "*Oh God, oh God, oh God!*"

Jenny pulled back and peered up at her friend, watching the look of ecstasy wash over her face as she quivered over the bed. When Niki finally dropped her hips back down onto the mattress, Jenny turned the vibrator off and straddled her hips, kissing her passionately.

"*Fuck*, that was hot," she said, nibbling Niki's ear. "I knew you'd enjoy these things."

"Not nearly as much as I like *you*," Niki said, grabbing Jenny's ass and pulling her closer as she pressed her tits against Jenny's breasts. "Can we put away the toys now and just concentrate on touching each other?"

"I thought you'd never ask," Jenny smiled, grinding her pussy against Niki's bare mound.

"I love the feeling of your body up against me," Niki panted. "I want to feel you fucking me *straight up* this time. I'm so wet right now."

"I can tell," Jenny said, sliding her body down Niki's abdomen, pressing her thighs apart until her chest rested against Niki's vulva.

"Rub your tits against me, Jenny," Niki pleaded, squirming her hips against Jenny's mounds.

Jenny raised herself up a few inches and grasped one of her globes with two hands, rubbing it playfully up and down Niki's slit.

Up to this point I'd just been rubbing my Lelo vibrator gently against my opening as I absent-mindedly watched the two girls interact. But when I saw Jenny tit-fucking her friend with her voluptuous breasts, I plunged the G-spot stimulator deep into my pussy, rolling it around as I moaned along with Niki.

"*Fuck*," she groaned. "That feels *way* better than a plastic vibrator. You're so warm and wet."

"You know what *also* feels warmer and wetter than a vibrator?" Jenny said, pushing Niki's knees up toward her chest, then lowering her hips over her friend's splayed pussy. As she placed her ass over Niki's twitching vulva, their pussies touched, and they groaned loudly.

"Jesus," Niki gasped. "Where did you learn to do this? Have you been holding out on me?"

"I've been studying a bit more than just math and chemistry since I've been here," Jenny purred, rolling her hips over Niki's upturned cunny.

"*Holy fuck!*" Niki groaned, feeling Jenny's clit pressing against her own. "This is the hottest thing I've ever done. I never even imagined–"

Jenny leaned forward, engulfing Niki's mouth with her own, pressing her tits against the other girl while the two of them ground their pussies together. I could hear the sexy slurping noises of their wet vulvas sliding over one another as their pink folds spread open for my camera. As they picked up the pace of their rocking motion, they moaned into each other's mouths and Niki wrapped her arms around Jenny's back, digging her fingernails into her skin.

Moments later, they both began squealing as their hips trembled in unison. I zoomed in as far as the camera would go, and just as Niki let out a high-pitched scream, Jenny began squirting all over her friend's perineum as Niki's rosebud puckered in and out. In all my years of watching lesbian trib videos, I'd never seen anything so sexy and raw. As I lay exhausted, drenched in my own pool of cum, I reached over and patted the sheet beside me.

If only you were here with me, I thought, imagining Jenny's body merging with my *own* instead of her friend's. *This trip to paradise isn't be complete without you.*

6

N iki went home the following day and for the rest of my vacation I watched old clips of Jenny playing with my toys. She'd occasionally take out a new one and pleasure herself on my bed or while watching lesbian videos, but I soon longed to be next to her, touching her directly. As I neared the end of my trip, I feared I'd lose her forever once the break was over, so I rescheduled my return flight and came home a day early.

When I got to the front door, I didn't feel comfortable barging in on her unannounced, so I tapped the doorbell. She came to the door wrapped in a large bath towel, and her eyes widened as she paused in the doorway.

"Mrs. Jackson!" she said. "I wasn't expecting you until tomorrow. Is everything okay?"

"Yes," I said, feeling Oscar rubbing himself against the bottom of my leg. "I was just feeling a bit sorry for you having to look after this big house all by yourself. I figured you could use an extra day getting ready to return to school."

"I've been studying hard," Jenny said, "so you needn't have worried. But come in out of the cold–it's your house after all."

"I didn't want to just barge in unannounced. I hope I didn't interrupt you in the middle of anything..."

"Actually, I was just getting ready to take another dip in your pool. It's been such a pleasure enjoying the heated water during the cool evenings."

I smiled, peering at Jenny's hourglass figure in the towel.

"And the hot tub too, I hope. It's a singular pleasure soaking in the stimulating bath when it's cold outside."

"Absolutely," Jenny nodded. "Your place is like a virtual playground for a starved teenager like me."

"Tell you what," I said. "Why don't I drop off my stuff in the bedroom and join you there in a few minutes? I could use another dip in the warm water to ease my transition back to the Chicago weather."

"Sure," Jenny said, noticing my erect nipples in my linen blouse from the chill outside. "Should I get changed?"

"It's starting to get dark, so the neighbors shouldn't be able to spy on us. I don't know about you, but I always enjoy soaking in the hot tub in the raw. It's just us girls, after all."

"I agree," Jenny smiled. "I'll meet you there in a few minutes."

I rushed upstairs and tore off my clothes, then threw on a robe and headed downstairs. When I opened the door to the veranda, Jenny had already submerged herself in the tub, and she peered up at me with dripping hair.

"You certainly look like you've made yourself at home," I smiled, dropping my robe and stepping into the swirling water a few feet away from her.

"It's been kind of fun, actually," she said. "I almost don't want to go back home. I could get used to hanging around here a little longer."

My heart skipped a beat, wondering if I should ask her to stay another night.

"Did you have any trouble operating any of the equipment?" I said, making a veiled reference to my sex toy collection. "Has everything been okay with the pool, the car, and other devices?"

"Yes," Jenny smiled. "Good on all fronts. Were you able to check in periodically to make sure I wasn't burning your house down?"

"Once in a while," I said. "I didn't want to interfere with your privacy too much. Mostly just to check that you were safe and well stocked up."

"I've been able to keep everything replenished pretty well," Jenny nodded. "Thanks to the use of your car. Thanks again for letting me have the use it."

"My pleasure," I said. "Have you been able to get out and see many of your friends while I was away?"

"Not too much," Jenny said. "I had a friend come over for a sleep-over one night to help break up the monotony."

"Did you show her around and avail yourselves of all the amenities?" I said, resisting the temptation to let her know just how much I knew she'd enjoyed that sleepover.

"Yes," Jenny blinked. "We went for a swim, had a relaxing hot tub–"

"Did you discover the special *nozzle*?" I smiled.

"You mean–"

"The one that sprays in a particularly delightful place."

"It was hard *not* to," Jenny blushed. "Once you find the right spot, you don't exactly want to move."

"And your *friend*? Did she discover it too?"

"Yes, but I think she was a bit self-conscious about trying it in my presence. I think that's something meant to be enjoyed more by yourself..."

"I don't know about *that*," I said, shifting my body over in front of the spigot. "I kind of missed this while I was away. Do you mind–?"

"Not at all," Jenny smiled. "After all, it's just us girls, right?"

"Right," I said, spreading my legs apart and shifting my weight forward to direct the spray onto my buzzing clit. "Mmm, yes–this is one luxury they didn't have at my expensive resort in Bora Bora."

"It must have been fun though," Jenny said, watching the expression on my face as I squirmed under the water. "There must have been lots of other exciting things to do there."

"I guess so," I said, catching my breath. "Snorkeling, sailing, swimming in the lagoon. It gets pretty old though when you're by yourself. I found myself checking in with you just to keep myself company."

"I hope you didn't catch me skinny dipping in your pool."

"I did indeed," I panted. "And in the hot tub. It looked like you were enjoying yourself as much as I am right now."

"I thought *maybe* you were watching me," Jenny said. "I caught the cameras pointed in my direction a few times."

"Did you *like* being watched?" I said.

"Sometimes," Jenny said. "It was kind of *stimulating* to be honest, knowing you were catching me occasionally without any clothes on."

"Oh yes," I groaned. "I caught you more than once."

"Did you enjoy watching me as much as I liked the idea of you watching me?" Jenny said, lifting an eyebrow.

"You have no idea," I panted. "Almost as much as I am right now."

"Mmm," Jenny said, dipping her hands below the surface of the water and shifting her weight on the seat opposite me. "I wish I could have spied on *you* as much as you were with me. You know, I always kind of had a thing for you, even when I was little. I always thought you were the most beautiful woman I'd ever seen."

"Oh my God, Jenny," I said, getting even more turned on knowing she found me attractive. "You've blossomed into the most beautiful, sexy young adult. *You're* the one I've had a crush on since you came over to my place."

"Oh Mrs. Jackson," Jenny panted, her cheeks beginning to flush.

"I think it's time you started calling me Jade," I smiled. "Seeing as how we're both stimulating ourselves under the water while watching each other."

"Jade," Jenny purred. "You have no idea how often I've fantasized about you."

"I must have come a hundred times thinking about you while I was away," I said. "I've wanted to feel your body against mine practically from the moment I left."

"Yes," Jenny moaned. "You're going to make me cum watching you."

"Yes, baby," I hissed. "Let it go. I'm almost there too."

"Uhnn," Jenny groaned, spreading her mouth wide open as she looked at me with glazed eyes.

Suddenly, I felt a bolt of electricity running through me as my orgasm washed over me. While we jerked and moaned together in simultaneous climax under the swirling water, we couldn't take our eyes off each other.

"Oh my God," Jenny panted after we both calmed down. "That was *so* hot."

"Let's get the hell out of here and go upstairs where we can do this *properly*," I said. "I need to feel a *warm body* next to me, not just an artificial water jet."

"I was thinking exactly the same thing," Jenny smiled.

The two of us scampered out of the hot tub and ran upstairs, giggling like two girls. When we got to the bed, I didn't even bother to pull down the covers, pulling her onto the mattress with me and entangling our legs together. It was electrifying feeling her naked body rubbing against mine, and for the longest time I was content to rub our slippery bodies together while we kissed passionately. The feeling of Jenny's big tits pressing against mine was sublime, and I was in no hurry to get down to more serious business.

But after a while, I felt Jenny's hands roaming lower on my body, and when her hand slipped into the cleft under my ass, I pulled back and looked at her.

"Jenny," I panted. "You have no idea how much I've wanted to feel your touch on my body."

"And yours on mine," Jenny grinned.

When she slipped two fingers into my hole, I squeezed her tits with two hands, pinching her large teats with my fingers.

"Uhnn," I groaned, feeling my juices spreading all over her hand. "I want to fuck you so bad."

"Yes please," Jenny said.

I pulled her hand out of my pussy, then pushed her down onto the bed and straddled her crotch with my thighs on either side of her hips.

"Does this position look familiar?" I said.

Jenny's eyes widened as she peered up at me with a look of shock.

"*No way!* You weren't watching me and my girlfriend when we were in your bedroom?!"

"I hope you don't mind," I nodded. "You did leave the door open just enough for my camera to zoom in from down the hallway."

"I was kind of hoping you were," Jenny smiled. "Did you see us playing with your toys too?"

"Absolutely," I grinned. "Your girlfriend is almost as hot as you are."

"Maybe the three of us can try this sometime," Jenny said. "I think she's become attracted to girls as much as I have since I've been here."

"Maybe another time," I said. "Right now, I just want to look at your magnificent body while I fuck you with my pussy."

"Yes, Jade," Jenny purred. "Fuck me with your pussy. I want to feel you cumming against me this time."

I rolled Jenny onto her side, pulling her right leg up onto my chest, then I tilted my hips forward until our pussies touched.

"Oh God," Jenny gasped. "Your pussy feels so hot."

"As hot as your *girlfriend's*?"

"It's *different* with you," she said. "I've never–"

"Been on the bottom before?" I smiled.

"Not like this," she said. "I *like* being fucked by you."

As I mashed my pussy into hers, I heard the familiar sloshing sound of our wet vulvas sucking and caressing each other's lips. I grabbed her tits with my two hands and squeezed them as hard as I could, feeling my ass slide over her slick thigh as we rocked our hips together.

"Jade," Jenny growled, peering at me with wild eyes. "I'm going to cum. Oh God, I'm going to cum all over your hot pussy."

Suddenly, I felt her hips shaking underneath me as a sexy flush rolled over her face.

"Yes, Jenny," I panted. "You're so beautiful. I'm going to cum with you, baby. Oh *fuck*–"

I pulled Jenny's upturned leg hard against my chest, feeling my pussy beginning to pulse in powerful contractions. Unable to hold it any longer, I gushed all over her slit as we wailed in delirious union. After what seemed like an eternity shaking and looking into each other's eyes while we enjoyed a long climax together, I collapsed onto the bed beside her and stroked her pretty face with the back of my hand.

"That was incredible," Jenny panted. "I don't think I've cum that hard in my whole life."

"Not even with my *Rabbit* vibrator or that funny finger-shaped sex toy?"

"Those were pretty good, I have to admit," she smiled. "But nothing like feeling your body next to mine." She looked between our legs at the huge wet spot that had formed on top of the comforter. "Plus, you've got a *special* power that none of those other devices have. That was the most stimulating shower I've had in a long time."

"There's more where that came from," I said, grinning like a Cheshire Cat. "Are you ready to try this again in a more equally yoked position?"

"Yes, but how would that work exactly?" Jenny asked. "Doesn't one of us kind of have to take the lead role when we're connected that way?"

I reached over and swung open my nightstand drawer, pulling out the long double-sided pink dildo.

"Not if something *else* is connecting us together," I smiled. "Have you had a chance to try *this* one yet?"

"I was kind of saving that one for you," Jenny said. "I figured you'd be able to show me how to use it properly."

"You got that right, girl," I smirked. "Now get up on all fours while I fuck you from behind with this thing."

"I like the sound of that," Jenny purred.

As I pressed one end of the dildo into my sopping hole and pressed my ass backwards towards hers, I tilted my head down and peered between my legs at her swinging tits.

This was one holiday I'd never soon forget, I thought to myself.

VOLUME FIVE

THE SLAVE

1

I always looked forward to my weekly lunch date with my best
friend and professional sex therapist, Hannah. But today, I had
a different reason for wanting to see her. My sex life had
become a bit staid and boring lately, and I wanted some new ideas for
how to spice things up. As a newly liberated, polysexual woman, I'd
had plenty of variety in my relationships, but I was tired of being the
one always taking the lead seeking out new adventures. I wanted
someone *else* to be in charge of plotting my sexual journey for a
change.

I smiled when I saw Hannah waiting in the foyer of the trendy
new Chicago restaurant, *Girl & the Goat*. Besides being my best friend
and a font of sexual knowledge, she was super-hot, and my pussy
tingled remembering our last tryst in the bushes behind the public
library.

"Funny you chose *this* place for our meet-up this week," I said,
kissing her gently on the cheek.

"How so?" she said. "I thought you'd like it, with its vegan menu
and convenient location next to the 'el'.

"No, it's not that. It's the name: Girl & the Goat. Given your profes-
sion and everything, it sounds like some kind of weird kink."

"Ha," Hannah chuckled. "It's certainly provocative, but I suspect it has more to do with the executive chef being a woman, and her proclivity toward farm-to-table food."

"Either way," I said, licking my lips. "As long as *you're* somewhere in the mix, I'm sure it will be super tasty."

After we sat down and ordered our entrees and some cocktails, Hannah rested her elbows on the table and leaned over toward me.

"What's up, girl?" she said, scrunching her eyebrows in concern. "You sounded a little down-in-the-dumps when I chatted with you last time over the phone."

"I dunno," I said. "I just feel like I'm in a bit of a rut. You know, *relationship*-wise."

"Are we talking about your *love* life or your *sex* life?" she said, smiling toward the waiter as he placed our drinks on the table.

"You know me," I laughed, taking a healthy swig of my margarita. "I'm still not ready for another long-term relationship after my last failed marriage. My sex life just feels kind of–predictable–lately."

Hannah suddenly hunched forward, coughing as she took a sip of her cosmopolitan.

"*Predictable?*" she said. "This coming from the girl who just came off a fling with the First Lady of the United States?!"

"That was a little different, I grant you. It's just that in most of my recent relationships, *I've* been the one taking the lead. I'm kind of getting tired having to take the first step and always being the one in charge in the bedroom department. Sometimes a girl just wants to be a lady, you know what I mean?"

"You mean being the *submissive* one for a change?" she said.

"I guess so. *You're* the sex therapist. Does there always have to be a top and a bottom, for want of a better expression, in every sexual relationship?"

Hannah paused while the waiter returned with our entrees, placing them in front of us on our place settings.

"That's the age-old question," she said, picking up one of her goat-cheese empanadas and chomping into it. "Traditionally, there's always been one dom and one submissive is most pair-bonds. I think it's a natural outgrowth of the old hunter-gatherer role of the male in a traditional heterosexual relationship and the homemaker/child-rearing role of the woman."

"Haven't we outgrown those old stereotypes in this modern enlightened age?" I said, shaking my head.

"You'd think so. But it seems to run deeper than that. Maybe it's a more visceral impulse, like with the alpha-beta-omega dynamic in a wolf pack. Whether they're hetero, gay, or lesbian, most couples naturally seem to assume one role or the other. With gays, it takes the form of 'tops' and 'bottoms' and with lesbians there's usually a 'butch' and a 'femme.'"

"But aren't these roles becoming more *fluid* these days with couples swapping positions from time to time?"

"Yes, of course," Hannah said, washing down her empanada with another gulp of her cosmo. "But each person seems to revert back eventually to their preferred position in the hierarchy. This seems like an odd question coming from such a sexually liberated person like yourself. It seems like you've tried just about *everything*. In fact, if I remember correctly, didn't you once avail yourself of the services of a professional dominatrix? Did you enjoy playing the submissive role in that situation?"

"Yes, but it all felt so manufactured, and temporary. Like I was *paying* to be dominated. It didn't feel natural."

Hannah shrugged her shoulders and chuckled.

"Well, you could pretty much walk into any lesbian bar in this town and find a dominant butch to take you on for a longer-term ride. With your pretty looks and that sexy body, you'd have no trouble picking up someone who's looking for some girly-girl fun."

"Mm, I don't know," I said, scrunching up my nose. "I'm not really attracted to that kind of woman. I guess I'm just looking for a 'normal' girl who I could experiment playing a more submissive role."

"What did you have in mind exactly?" Hannah said, leaning back in her chair.

"I don't know, someone pretty, kind of like *you*, who's not afraid to take the lead for a while..."

"Just how far did you want to take this whole submissive thing?" she said, arching an eyebrow.

"Whatever," I said, nibbling on one of my chickpea fritters. "I could go all-in, for a little while at least. It might be kind of fun, letting my partner have her way with me for a change."

"Hmm," Hannah purred, as a sly smile began to spread across her lips.

"*What?*" I said. "What are you thinking all of a sudden?"

"It's been a while since the two of us have had a roll in the hay, so to speak. Why don't we mix it up a little this time? I'll play the domme and you can be the submissive."

"That sounds like fun," I nodded, feeling my panties moistening at the thought of reconnecting with Hannah sexually. "But we've both had plenty of turns being the one on top–"

"No," she said. "I mean in a more *formal* type of domme and submissive role."

"You mean like in a BDSM type of thing?"

"Kind of," she smiled. "I was thinking more in terms of a *master-and-slave* type of role."

I lifted my hand to my mouth, suddenly coughing on a chick pea. Now it was *my* turn to be surprised.

"You want me to be your *slave*?" I said. "What would that entail, exactly?"

"Whatever I deem necessary," she smirked. "Whatever I want you to do, *whenever* and *wherever* we might find ourselves."

"You mean like in public places too?"

"Yes," Hannah nodded. "If the mood strikes me."

"That sounds kind of fun," I said, suddenly squirming in my chair at the thought of being at Hannah's behest whenever she demanded. "When did you want to start this little experiment?"

"How about right *now*?" Hannah said, peering at me with a devilish grin.

2

"Okay..." I said, suddenly intrigued. "What did you have in mind exactly?"

"I want you to get under the table and eat my pussy."

"Right *here*? Right *now*? There must be a hundred people in this place, and we're only separated by a few feet!"

Hannah peered at me as a slight curl formed in the corner of her lip.

"I'm going to get up and create a distraction. When you see the right opportunity, duck under the table. Nobody should notice with everything else that's going on. And the long table covering should disguise you while you're under there."

"What about when I need to get *out*?" I said, wrinkling my forehead in dismay.

"We'll figure that out when the time comes," Hannah said. "Now get ready. You won't have much time to make your move when the opportunity presents."

"Are you sure this is a good idea–" I said, peering around me at all the restaurant patrons talking amongst themselves mere inches away from us.

"Don't worry your pretty little head about it," she said, rising from her chair. "This shouldn't take long. I'll be back in a flash."

Hannah picked up her purse and began walking toward the restaurant washroom. As she approached a waiter carrying a tray of food on his shoulder, she peered down into her purse, pretending to look for something. Suddenly, she tripped toward the waiter, and he stumbled, dropping the tray of food and beverages onto the floor with a noisy clatter.

"Oh my God!" Hannah cried, pretending to be just as surprised as the shaken waiter. "I'm so sorry. I was just looking for something in my purse–"

"Not to worry," the waiter said, bending down to pick up the fallen dishes and broken glasses on the floor. "These things happen more often than you can imagine around here. Are you alright? Did I spill anything on you?"

While the two of them continued their discussion, I glanced around me, and noticing that all eyes had turned temporarily toward the distraction on the other side of the restaurant, I flipped up the table covering and ducked underneath, feeling my heart pounding like a freight train.

I could hear Hannah and the waiter talking in the distance, then things slowly quieted down as the normal hum of chatter of the lunch guests talking and the kitchen staff working resumed. After a few minutes, Hannah returned to the table, placing her purse on the floor beside her and sitting down quietly in her chair. Fortunately for both of us, she'd chosen to wear a mid-length skirt today that provided ready access to her lower region while providing a modicum of cover from the surrounding restaurant guests.

Hannah slowly spread her legs apart and I could see in the dim light under the table a small wet spot in the middle of her sheer panties. Smiling at the ingenuity of her brilliant ruse, I reached under her skirt and threaded my thumbs under the top of her panties, slowly pulling them down to her ankles. I could see her bald pussy glistening from the moisture that had accumulated on her tumescent labia, and I paused for a moment admiring her pretty vulva.

"Ahem," Hannah coughed above me, strumming her fingers impatiently on the table.

Taking her cue to proceed, I spread her legs further apart and pressed my face between the gap, slowly licking the inside of her quivering thighs. Although I was nominally the submissive one in this unusual situation, that didn't mean I couldn't tease her for a bit and enjoy a certain degree of control while I followed her bidding.

As I moved my face closer to her steaming pussy, she shifted her hips forward, pressing her pubis toward my mouth. When I felt her wet slit touch my lips, I extended my tongue and slid it gently between her folds. Hannah groaned softly as she scrunched down lower in her chair, and I moved my hands under her skirt to grab the sides of her cheeks, pulling her harder into my face. As she slowly began to undulate her hips against my face, I raised my head, drawing a line upward between her dripping slit toward her exposed bulb. I could see it peeking out of its hood now, like a ripe cherry dangling on a tree.

Hannah flapped her thighs in and out around the sides of my head, and I could tell she was growing impatient for me to take her into my mouth. Realizing that we'd have a limited amount of time to consummate this act, I open my lips and sucked her gland into my mouth, rolling my tongue over her hardened shaft.

Hannah lurched forward and moaned as the dinnerware shook on the table above me. Feeling newly empowered by tormenting her while the rest of the restaurant patrons went about their business oblivious to what was happening mere inches away, I snaked my right hand up between her thighs and thrust two fingers into her tight hole. She gripped the sides of the table with her two hands, trying to maintain her composure in the packed lunchroom. Suddenly, I heard some footsteps approach our table and the sound of our waiter's voice talking to Hannah.

"I see that you've finished your main course," he said. "Would you like something for dessert?"

Hannah peered up at him with glazed eyes.

"Oh, um–sure," she said, clamping my face between her legs

trying to stop me from what I was doing while she spoke to the waiter.

"What do you have on offer?" she said, too distracted to look at the menu.

"Today's special is French silk pie or our signature Girl & the Goat cupcakes."

"The cupcakes sound fine, thank you," Hannah said.

"And for your *friend*?" the waiter said, peering at my half-finished plate of fritters. "Will she be rejoining you soon?"

I smiled as I listened to Hannah pretend like everything was normal while I continued curling my fingers inside her throbbing pussy toward her G-spot. She coughed as she jerked in her chair, trying to suppress the pleasure that was rapidly consuming her body.

"She just had to freshen up in the washroom," she said to the waiter. "I'm sure she'll join us again shortly. We'll order her dessert when she returns."

"As you wish," the waiter said. "I'll be back in a few minutes."

"Thank you," Hannah squeaked, her voice suddenly breaking from the feeling of my hands and fingers caressing her under the table.

When the waiter left, Hannah spread her legs further apart and she reached under the table, pulling my head toward her pussy firmly with one hand.

"You better get this over with fast," she whispered. "Before the waiter comes back and begins to wonder what happened to you. Besides, you're driving me crazy. I need to get off soon or I'll never be able to finish my meal."

Feeling just as eager to bring her to climax in full view of the other restaurant patrons, I stepped up the pace of my licking and sucking, drawing her button hard into my mouth.

"Yes, baby," Hannah purred. "Suck my pussy. I'm going to come in your mouth with everybody watching. You're being such a good little slave."

Hannah's dirty talk was turning me on almost as much as it must have been for her, and I squeezed her ass tightly imagining what it must have felt like to have someone licking your pussy surrounded by so many people. Her hips began to shake and I could hear her panting more rapidly above me over the table. I pushed my fingers harder up inside her, pressing my knuckles hard against her dripping slit while I flicked my tongue over her clit and curled my fingers against her G-spot.

Suddenly, Hannah grabbed the sides of my head with two hands and pulled my face tightly against her splayed legs as her hips buckled against my head. I could hear her groaning softly above me while she tried to suppress the waves of pleasure rolling over her as her pussy clamped down over my fingers in a series of powerful contractions. I held her nub in my mouth, feeling the walls of her pussy contracting around my fingers until her hips stopped quivering and her buttock muscles slowly relaxed. After giving her a moment to recover from her orgasm, I pulled my fingers out of her pussy and sat back on the heels of my feet under the table.

"What *now*?" I whispered to her through the draped tablecloth. "How am I going to get out of here now?"

"I don't know," Hannah said. "I don't think I can get away with another waiter distraction. Maybe you can just roll out of there pretending like you dropped something."

Hannah reached into her purse and tossed her compact onto the floor beside me. I picked it up and hesitated for a moment, then I flung the side of the tablecloth aside and rolled out from under the table, trying to appear as nonchalant as possible.

"I knew I'd dropped this thing *somewhere*," I said, holding up the compact to the startled guests sitting next to our table, then sitting down on my chair like nothing unusual had happened.

"Well *that* was invigorating," I said, smiling at Hannah as the lunch guests resumed their usual discourse.

"I'll say," she said, reaching down to pull up her panties. "I practically burst a gasket when the waiter came by at the worst possible moment. You weren't very helpful when you didn't take my cue to stop stimulating me while I pressed my thighs against your head."

"Oh *come on*," I said, smiling at her with a fiendish grin. "I couldn't let *you* be the only one having all the fun."

"Maybe so," she grinned, her face still flushed from the after-effects of her recent climax. "But it looks like I'm going to have to teach you a little more discipline about what it means to be a proper sex slave."

"Oh?" I said, raising a playful eyebrow. "What did you have in mind next for me?"

"You're going to have to wait until we finish our meal," she said, noticing the waiter approaching our table once again.

"Here are your cupcakes, ma'am," he said, placing a dish with two cupcakes on the placemat in front of her. Then he turned toward me, nodding toward my unfinished main course. "Were you finished with your entree, ma'am? Perhaps you'd like something for desert also?"

I paused for a moment, peering over at Hannah playfully while I glanced down at her plate.

"I'll have whatever *she's* having," I said, picking up one of her cupcakes and mashing it into my mouth as the icing dripped around the edges of my mouth.

3

———————

After lunch, Hannah drove me back to her place, but she wouldn't tell me what she had in store for me next. When we pulled into her driveway, she led me out of the car and up her stairs into her master bathroom. Without saying a word, she turned on the large glass-enclosed shower and began to undress me. As the room began to fill with the warm mist from the running water, I looked over at her with a puzzled expression.

"What are you planning to do with me now?" I said. "Give me a golden shower?"

"That wasn't my intent," she said. "But now that you mention it, that's not a bad idea. No, I have some *other* dirty ideas in mind for you. But first I need to get us cleaned up in preparation for the next step in your education as a slave."

"Mmm, I like the sound of that," I smiled. "Are you coming in the shower with me?"

"Mm, hmm," Hannah nodded. "But don't get too excited. This is all about attending to *my* needs, not the other way around."

"That's okay," I said. "Just being in the shower naked with you will satisfy my needs for the rest of the day."

After Hannah removed the rest of my clothes, she disrobed and the two of us stepped into the warm spray of the shower.

"Mmm, this is delightful," I said, sliding my naked body against hers as the water began to coat our slippery bodies.

"The first rule about being a slave is no *touching* unless otherwise instructed," she said, pushing me away. "Now pick up the bar of soap and give me a proper cleansing, and I mean *everywhere*."

"Okay..." I said, picking up the jasmine-scented bar of soap from the soap dish and beginning to rub it over Hannah's shoulders and tits.

"That's a good slave," she purred. "I want you to rub every square inch of me—and don't forget all the hidden crevasses."

"It'll be my pleasure," I said, ogling Hannah's glistening body under the bright light of the shower.

As instructed, I was careful to roll the soap over every part of her body, starting at the top and working my way downward. When I reached her mound, I felt the bar of soap sticking for a moment on the short stubble of her pubis, and the bar fell onto the floor.

"Sorry, Hannah," I said, bending down to retrieve the bar.

"That's okay," she said, peering at my upturned butt as I leaned over at the waist. "I kind of prefer you from this angle anyway. But from now on, I want you to refer to me as Master. I will refer to you simply as Slave."

Hannah slapped my ass hard from behind and I lurched forward, almost losing my footing on the slippery floor. Then she reached between my legs and clamped her hand around my upturned mound with a firm grip, pulling me toward her.

"Do you *like* it when I play rough with you, Slave?"

Mmm, yes, Master," I sputtered as the water streamed down my back and flowed over the front of my face.

Hannah slapped my other butt cheek hard before instructing me to resume my cleaning ritual.

"Now stand up and finish the job. You still haven't finished cleaning my lower regions."

"Yes, Master," I said, repositioning myself in front of her and rolling the bar of soap over her mound and between her legs toward her perineum.

"Yes," Hannah jerked, feeling the slippery bar sliding over her sensitive parts. "Just like that. I want you to give my private parts extra special attention."

"Yes, Master," I smiled, angling the bar between her folds and rubbing it softly over the base of her mound where her clit poked out, aroused by the combination of the slippery soap rubbing against her and the warm water streaming between her legs.

But just as I was getting into lavishing her pussy with the slippery bar, she turned around and tilted her ass up with her hands resting on the side of the shower wall.

"Now clean my pucker too," she instructed. "I want to feel you caressing *every* part of me."

"Mmm," I hummed, only too happy to touch the most private parts of her body.

I separated her butt cheeks, then slowly ran the bar of soap between her crack, caressing her rosebud with the tips of my fingers.

"Yes," she panted. "I like the touch of your fingers on my butthole. Now coat your fingers with some soap and insert two of them inside me."

"In your *anus*?" I said, shocked at the audacity of her invitation.

"Yes," she said. "Just a little way, up to the first knuckle or so. I want to see what it feels like to have you rim me with your fingers."

I rolled the bar of soap in my hands then pressed my forefinger and middle finger slowly into her sphincter, being careful to keep my nails pointed upward so as not to pinch her sensitive tissue.

"*Fuck* yes," Hannah hissed, pressing her ass back toward me to meet the pressure of my probing fingers. "Now curl them around in there a little bit like when you finger my pussy."

As I began to gently move my fingers around in her butthole, I was surprised how much of a turn-on it was for me. This was something I'd never really explored before, and there was something very sexy and raunchy about pegging my girlfriend from behind, even if it *was* just with the tips of my fingers. Her sphincter was tighter than I imagined, and I felt my pussy throbbing under the warm flow of water splashing over the two of us while I probed her from behind.

"That's enough," she suddenly said, tilting her hips forward and making a plopping sound as my fingers popped out of her hole. "Now wash your hands with the bar of soap and rinse the rest of my perineum before cleaning my legs and feet."

While I followed Hannah's instructions, I slowly bent down at my knees, moving further and further down her body until I reached her feet. She lifted up one foot then the other, giving me access to the bottom of her soles, then she grabbed my wet hair, pulling my face hard into her open pussy. I choked for a moment from the combined pressure of her wet flesh covering my nose and mouth and from the cascade of water pouring down over her stomach onto my upturned face. But instead of giving me a chance to continue licking and sucking her pussy as in the restaurant, after a few seconds she pulled my head back and peered down at me while I blinked up at her under the spray of falling water.

"That's a good slave," she smiled. "I think we're finished in here. Now get up and fetch me a towel to dry me off."

"Yes, Master," I said, disappointed that she wasn't going to give me a chance to finish the job I'd started.

I scrambled out of the shower and tip-toed over the wet floor to retrieve a bath towel from the towel rack, then Hannah stepped out of the shower and turned around while I patted her dry.

"That'll do," Hannah said, taking the towel from me and walking over to the padded stool in front of her make-up mirror. "Now I want you to attend to some personal grooming. Get on your knees on the floor while I gather the necessary tools."

What kind of tools did she have in mind? I thought. *She's really getting into this whole role-playing scenario.*

But it didn't bother me since I was actually enjoying this little role reversal and eager to see what she had in mind next. I bent down on the wet tile floor, wondering why she hadn't allowed me to towel myself dry, feeling the residual water from the shower dripping out of my hair down the middle of my back and over the crack of my ass. I shivered from the sensation, not because I was cold, but from the feeling of the warm water caressing my splayed labia and tingling clit, now fully exposed from my heightened state of arousal.

When Hannah returned, she placed a women's razor and a tube of shave gel on the floor beside me, then she sat down on the stool, spreading her legs wide in front of my face.

"It's been a while since I've shaved my pussy," she said. "It's getting a little rough down there. I want you to shave me nice and smooth, just like you are."

Hannah knew that I'd undergone laser treatment to remove every trace of hair from my perineum area, but she'd been holding off having similar treatment for fear of the pain involved in the procedure.

"And you better be careful not to cut or nick me down there, or there'll be severe consequences."

"Yes ma'am—er, *Master*," I said, squeezing a dollop of gel onto my hands and rubbing it gently over her scruffy mound and stubbly labia.

It took me a good thirty minutes to finish shaving her, especially the super-sensitive area on the sides of her vulva and along her perineum between her pussy and her asshole. Although I was nervous about cutting her at various times, the act of shaving her most private regions with a sharp blade while I stared at her dripping pussy was a tremendous turn on. I could feel my own juices running down the insides of my thighs while I smiled at Hannah's inflamed clit and tumescent lips as I carefully trimmed her stubble.

When I finished, she picked up a hand-held mirror from the vanity table and angled it toward her snatch, admiring my handiwork.

"You did a good job, Slave," she smiled, rubbing her hand over her smooth-as-velvet skin. "There might be a little reward in this for you later if you continue to be a good girl. But first, there's one other grooming job I want you to attend to while you're down there."

Hannah fetched another bag of items from one of the drawers, then unzipped the bag and handed me a nail file.

"I haven't done my *nails* in a while either," she said. "I want you to file them down a quarter of an inch and make them just as smooth as my pussy."

I took one look at the length of her nails and furrowed my forehead.

"Have you got some clippers? It's going to take quite a while to sand them down that much–"

Hannah grabbed my wet hair and pulled my face up to meet her angry gaze.

"Remember who's in *charge* here," Hannah said. "I want you to take your time and do them the professional way. And don't talk back to your master like that. You've got to learn your position as my slave. Now get to work."

As I lifted one of Hannah's feet and began sanding her toenails with the nail file, I began to wonder if this whole dom and submissive thing was still a good idea. She seemed to be getting a little too seriously into the role. She was no longer the happy-go-lucky, always-joking-around best friend I remembered. I figured I'd entertain her with this little escapade for another couple of hours or so. Then I'd be happy to revert back to my usual role taking the lead in my sexual affairs.

But as I looked up at Hannah with doleful eyes, she peered down and winked at me with a lopsided smile.

I guess she's just getting into character, I thought. *Let's see how far she wants to take this thing. Maybe she's trying to teach me a lesson.*

As I caressed her soft feet, I glanced up at her newly shaven pussy and noticed a dribble of lubrication dripping out of her hole and down the crack of her ass. I peered back up at her and winked with my opposite eye.

Yin and Yang. Tops and bottoms. Domme and femme. Maybe this was the natural way of the world after all.

4

———————

After I finished Hannah's pedicure, she leaned over and towel-dried my hair then patted me down to remove the last vestiges of water remaining on my back. Then she held out her hand and raised me off my knees, leading me toward the bedroom. When we got to her large four-poster bed, we stopped and I looked at her expectantly, hoping we'd finally have a chance to connect and have sex like we used to. Instead, she just looked at me blankly then pushed me backwards over the foot of the bed, where I toppled onto her mattress face up with my legs spread apart.

"Perfect," she said. "Stay in that position while I collect a few things for our next act."

Hannah fished through her chest of drawers, then returned with a jumble of scarves, placing them on the bed beside me.

"Mmm," I said, smiling at her with a raised eyebrow. "Are you going to blindfold me?"

"No," she said. "But you won't be needing your eyes for this next thing I have in mind. Or your *hands*, for that matter."

Hannah picked up one of the scarves and wound it around my right wrist, then she pulled my arm up to the corner of the bed near the headboard and tied the loose ends around one of the posts, double-tying the knot firmly. Then she went around to the other side of the bed and repeated the procedure, tying my other hand to the other post. As she walked down toward the foot of the bed, she looked at me with a sly smile then she grasped my two feet and pulled me forcefully toward her, stretching my arms out straight.

"Ow!" I said, more playfully than actually hurting in pain. "There's no need to be so rough with me."

"I'm sorry if I hurt your feelings," Hannah smirked. "Remember, this whole thing was *your* idea. You can stop it at any time you want by saying the magic word."

"You mean 'stop', or 'I don't want to play anymore'?"

"Either of those will do. You're always in charge of what happens to your body."

I peered up at her with a little girl pout, then smiled.

"No," I said. "I don't want you to stop. I just want you to remember who you're playing with here. Someday the tables might be turned around the other way."

"Oh, I *definitely* know what I'm playing with," Hannah said as she tied my two feet to the bottom bedposts, admiring my naked body spread-eagled on top of her mattress. "And I plan to take maximum advantage of it while I have the chance."

She crawled up onto the mattress from the base of the bed and kneeled between my legs, running her eyes up and down my figure.

"You look absolutely delectable in this position, Jade," she said, her eyes widening at the prospect of ravishing me in my helpless state. "I'm going to take my time getting off this time while you caress and nibble every part of my body."

"That might be kind of hard to do in my current predicament," I said, thrashing my hands and feet to remind her of my limited mobility.

"That's okay," she said. "You're not going to need any of those extra appendages with what I'm planning to do to you. Everything except your *mouth*, that is. I have special plans for *that* part of your anatomy."

"Mmm," I purred, happy to have a chance to lick her body again.

"Well then, scooch right on up here. I'll be happy to eat your pussy while you sit on my face–"

"All in good time, my dear," she said. "But first, there's a few *other* parts of your body I'd like to play with."

Hannah lifted one of her knees and straddled my left thigh, then lowered her pussy on top of my warm skin. I could feel her wetness coating my leg as she began to rock her hips against my flexing upper thigh muscle.

"Your skin feels so soft, Jade," she said, temporarily dispensing with the pejorative term she'd used for me previously. "You've done a nice job shaving my peachka nice and smooth. You feel exquisite against my skin."

"As do you, Han–I mean *Master*," I said. "I can feel your juices coating my leg."

"Yes," Hannah nodded. "I plan on leaving my mark all over you before I'm finished with you."

"Fuck, yes," I said, lifting my hips off the mattress, begging her to move her body closer to my aching snatch.

Hannah looked down at my bald pussy and licked her lips. Then she slowly dragged her dripping crotch over the length of my upper thigh, pausing when she reaching my apex. I could feel the warmth of her left thigh pressing up against my vulva, and I humped my hips, vainly trying to gain the necessary friction to stimulate my clit.

Noticing the desperation in my eyes, she lifted herself off me temporarily, then repositioned herself straddling my upper pelvis with her two legs. Then she lowered her wet pussy onto the top of my mound and proceeded to grind her clit against my hard pubic bone. She let out a deep guttural moan and I tried to angle my hips upward to gain traction on my own burning gland, but instead she pressed me back down onto the mattress, careful to position her pussy just out of reach of my tingling gland.

"You're *evil*, you know that?" I hissed, giving her a death stare.

"It's all part of the role, baby," she smiled. "You wanted to be the slave. It's your job to give *me* pleasure, not the other way around."

"*Fine*," I huffed. "I'm enjoying the show plenty enough as it is. In fact, I could probably get off just watching you rub your pussy against my muff."

"I suppose you could," Hannah said, knowing full well as a sex therapist about neurological phenomenon of referred pleasure and pain. "I guess we'll just have to find another way to stimulate my pussy then."

Hannah wiggled her body up higher on my torso, shifting her weight from one knee to the other until she reached my tits, which by now were swollen and distended from the intense stimulation I was experiencing. Then she lowered her dripping pussy onto one of my erect teats and proceeded to fuck my little phallus between her slippery labia.

"Oh my God," I hummed. "That feels incredible. Fuck my tit with your pretty pussy, Hannah."

"*Who?*" she said, glaring at me indignantly.

"I mean *Master*. Fuck me with your smooth pussy, Master. I want to watch you cum all over my big tits."

"I'd love to accommodate you, my dear," she smiled. "But I have other plans for cumming all over you."

She suddenly lifted herself up and turned her body around with her ass toward my head then slowly inched her gaping hole up toward my face.

"Yes," I panted. "Sit on my face. I want to suck on that nicely shaved pussy and flick my tongue all over that big bean."

"I think we can manage that," Hannah said, lowering her glistening crotch onto my eagerly awaiting mouth.

When I felt her slippery folds press against my face, I lapped up her juices like a hungry puppy dog. She pressed her pelvis hard against my jaw, and I could feel her hard button rubbing against the top row of my teeth. I spread my lips to give her maximum friction against the hard surface, and she began to rock her hips rapidly forward and back. The crack of her ass kept rubbing against my nose, but this only added to the excitement of the situation, especially as I inhaled the sweet smell of the jasmine still lingering on her skin.

While Hannah picked up the pace of her rocking and grinding, she bent forward and began licking my tits, wildly rimming my tingling nipples with her slathering tongue. As I watched her pretty pucker flexing inches away from my wide eyes, I began to feel the familiar pangs of an orgasm building up inside me. But once again, just as I was about to reach the crest of my pleasure, she lifted herself off me, holding her body inches away from my flapping tongue desperately trying to reach her inflamed clit.

"What the fuck, Hannah–" I started to object.

But I didn't have a chance to finish my complaint as she tilted her hips forward, planting her ass directly over my lips.

"Shut up and lick my asshole, Slave," she huffed. "There's plenty of *other* ways we can put that talented tongue to work."

At first, I was surprised by the temerity of Hannah's bold move, but as she began to spread her legs further apart and wiggle her ass on my face, I quickly forgot about what part of her body I was licking and began munching on her anus with unremitted abandon. There was no trace of any unpleasant smell or taste, only the warm feeling of her soft flesh in my mouth and the sweet smell of the jasmine body wash.

As Hannah began to moan in delight above me, I extended my tongue and probed her hole, rolling it around the edges and washing it with my warm saliva. I'd never licked a woman's asshole before, but I knew that it was a highly erogenous zone and that it was everyone's fantasy. And from the sound of Hannah's rapidly escalating whimpers and moans above me, it was obvious this was one of *Hannah's* too.

As she began to shake her hips more rapidly over my face and press her weight down harder onto my face, I could see her butt cheeks beginning to quiver in a state of imminent climax. When her orgasm finally hit her, Hannah wailed at the top of her lungs as her whole body shook like she was having an epileptic seizure. When I felt her sphincter pulsing in my mouth, I couldn't hold back any longer and I raised my hips high off the mattress, gushing like a faucet from my own powerful orgasm taking hold of me. For what seemed like an eternity, the two of us swiveled our hips wildly, locked in the most powerful orgasm either one of us had experienced in a long time.

Referred pleasure indeed, I thought as my orgasm slowly began to ebb. *Maybe I should try this role-play stuff more often.*

5

———————

When Hannah finally stopped shaking over top of my face, she lifted herself up and flopped down on the mattress beside me, breathing heavily.

"Holy *fuck*," I said. "Was that just me, or was that the most erotic, powerful orgasm I've had in a long time?"

"No," she panted. "You aren't kidding. I haven't cum that hard, since, well, the *last* time I was with you."

"Who knew the anus could be such a pleasure receptor?" I said, licking my tongue over my mouth to taste the remnants of her scent still on my lips.

"I guess the gay guys are on to something after all," she nodded.

I turned my head toward her and peered at her with a sly smile.

"That's the *real* reason you wanted me to wash you down there, isn't it? You had this whole thing planned right from the beginning."

"Maybe, she smirked. But the pussy shave and pedicure also helped to put me in the mood. I almost came watching you stare at my pussy while you filed my nails."

"You're such a bitch," I said, giving her a gentle nudge with my elbow.

"That's bitch-*Master*, to you," she grinned back at me.

"Yes Master," I nodded obsequiously. "So what now? Are you going to untie me and let me properly satisfy myself now? If I don't touch my clit soon, I'm going to explode."

"Maybe in a little while," Hannah said, giving me a devilish smile. "There's one last thing I wanted to do to you before we end this little submissive and dom thing."

"I can't imagine what else you could do to me that could be more defiling than rubbing your asshole into my face while I'm helplessly tied up."

"Oh, you have *no* idea," she said, getting up off the bed and heading back to her chest of drawers, where she retrieved a huge pink strap-on dildo.

"No *way!*" I said, shaking my head. "You weren't thinking of fucking me up the *ass* with that thing!?"

"Probably not," she smirked. "But I *do* like the idea of fucking you from behind with it."

Hannah placed the dildo on the bed and slowly untied each of my hands from the bedposts. Then she flipped me over and retied my hands in the same position, this time with me facing down onto the mattress.

"Holy shit, Hannah," I said. "Now I'm even more vulnerable than before. You can pretty much do whatever you want to me in this position."

"That's exactly the idea," she said, slowly strapping on the silicon dildo like she was a cowboy preparing for a gunslinging contest.

"Be careful with that thing," I said as she approached the side of the bed, estimating the length of the phallus at a good eight inches. "You could take someone's eye out with that thing if you're not too careful."

"Oh, don't worry," Hannah smiled. "I don't plan on going anywhere near your *face* with my pretty little cock. I've got some other plans for it. Now I'm *really* going to show you what it means to be a dom and a submissive."

Hannah hopped up on the bed straddling my hips and positioned her crotch directly above my bare ass cheeks. Then she rocked her hips up and down overtop of me, causing the flexible appendage attached to her harness to slap loudly against my buttocks.

"You said you wanted something to touch your pussy," she said. "Well get ready, because you're about to have the ride of your life."

"Yes, Master," I whinnied, tilting my ass up as much as my restraints allowed to give her freer access to my pussy.

For a long moment, Hannah paused inches above my ass with her weapon, and for a second I thought she was contemplating fucking me up the ass with it. But when I felt her grab the end of the dildo and swipe it gently up and down my quivering slit, I moaned in anticipation of her filling my aching cunt.

"Fuck me with your big dick, Master," I pleaded. "I need you to fill me up with your organ. I want to feel you inside me."

"Oh yes," Hannah grunted, positioning the tip of the phallus at the entrance to my dripping hole.

She pushed it in an inch or two, then paused for a moment before plunging it all the way inside my tight snatch.

"Uhn!" I grunted, feeling the probe pressing against the end of my cavity.

"Oh *God*, Hannah," I said, momentarily dispensing with the proper terms I was supposed to use in our little game of top and bottom. "Fuck me with that thing like there's no tomorrow."

"Damn *straight*, girl," Hannah hissed, equally lost in the moment.

As she lowered her body onto my back, I felt her cool tits rubbing against my shoulder blades while she began to pound her hips forcefully against my buttocks. With each thrust, I clenched my cheeks, reveling in the feeling of her hard mound pressing up against me. She was fucking me hard and deep enough that I could feel the base of the dildo ramming against my tingling clit, and I tilted my hips up a degree or two higher to generate more friction.

It didn't take long for the feelings of another powerful orgasm to well up inside me, and as we both slapped our hips together like two bucking broncos, our combined cries of ecstasy escalated in likewise fashion. At the crest of my pleasure, I cried out to Hannah to signal that I was about to come.

"I'm going to cum, Han. I'm going to cum hard all over your big cock. Ram that monster inside me while I gush all over you pussy."

"*Fuck* yes," Hannah grunted, pressing her hips hard against my ass in one final forceful thrust as her tits quivered against my back at the beginning of another strong orgasm.

When I felt her cumming on top of me, I couldn't hold back and longer and I screamed at the top of my lungs as my entire vulva began flexing and clamping in a series of powerful contractions while the built-up fluid inside my pussy began spraying out the sides of our tight connection all over Hannah's buckling thighs behind the leather of her strap-on harness.

When we both finally stopped cumming after waking up the entire neighborhood, Hannah collapsed on top of my back with the dildo still inserted deep inside me, resting her head softly against my throbbing heart. Even though she had me in the most compromised possible submissive and dominant position possible at this moment, I could feel the love and tenderness emanating from her body as she wrapped her arms tenderly around me, softly caressing the sides of my breasts.

6

———

Hannah pulled the dildo out of me, then we cuddled for a while and fell asleep atop her mattress for a couple of hours. When I woke up, I heard her foraging around in the kitchen and I went downstairs to see what she was up to. When I saw that she was preparing a pasta salad, I peered up at her with a quizzical expression.

"I thought your *slave* was supposed to do all the domestic work," I joked. "Shouldn't *I* be the one getting dinner ready?"

She turned toward me and smiled.

"I thought maybe you'd like to switch roles for a while," she said. "Aren't you growing tired of being the submissive one yet?"

"Not really," I said with a sheepish grin. "After that last experience, I'm kind of getting into it. It's kind of fun being the bottom for a change."

"Just how far do you want to go with this thing?" she said, spooning some of the salad into a bowl and sliding it across the kitchen island toward me.

"*You're* the one in charge here," I said. "Use your imagination. Surely there must be a few *other* ways you can think of to use and abuse me."

Hannah pulled up a chair beside me and sat down to eat her salad as her eyes flitted around trying to think of what to do next. After a few minutes, she peered up at me with a mischievous smile on her face.

"*What?*" I said. "What are you dreaming up now?"

"It seems to me that the obvious next step in your evolution as a slave is to test the waters with a few *other* players. How would you feel about my taking you to a lesbian bar?"

"That doesn't sound like too much of a stretch," I said. "It's not like I haven't picked up a girl in a bar before..."

"Not the kind of bar *I* have in mind. It's pretty hard-core. Plus, I have an idea how we could make it a little more interesting."

"Oh?" I said. "Do tell."

"I was thinking maybe we could dress you up in a provocative costume, something more befitting of your role as a slave. Then we could *really* test how strong this dominant-submissive impulse is in a natural setting."

"What, you mean like in some kind of tight leather outfit or something?"

"Something like that," Hannah smiled. "Why don't we go to our friend Cheryl's sex shop and try a few things on? She's got some pretty wild outfits in the back."

"Okay," I said, feeling my panties beginning to dampen at the idea of parading myself around a lesbian bar dressed up in an sexy outfit.

After dinner, Hannah and I drove to Cheryl's Babeland store on Broadway, where she escorted us to a fitting room in the back of the store. After talking with Cheryl about what we had in mind, she disappeared into the back and brought out a few outfits for me to try on. The first few garments involved the predictable see-through lingerie sets and skimpy schoolgirl costumes, but when she brought us a full-length vinyl body suit with strategic hole placements, both of our eyes widened in excitement. Decorated with metal studs and large fabric cut-outs for the breasts, buttocks and crotch area, it left little to the imagination.

After I tried it on, Hannah's eyes opened as wide as saucers while she nodded at me with a huge grin on her face. Somehow, wearing this full-length shiny body suit made me feel even *more* naked by drawing attention to my private areas.

"Holy shit," she said, admiring me in the full-length dressing room mirror. "That is one shit-hot, smoking outfit."

"You can't possibly imagine me walking into a *public setting* wearing this thing?" I said, shaking my head as I turned my body around to examine just how revealing it was on both sides of my body.

"Um, actually," she smiled. "I can. Can you imagine the kind of interest you'll generate walking into a lesbian bar dressed up like that? Talk about a *chick magnet*. You'd have every butch-dyke hitting on you in no time."

"Not to mention most of the *other* girls in the bar," Cheryl nodded, coming into the dressing room to inspect my outfit. "But if you *really* want to attract the dommes and take your role-playing to the next level, I have one *other* accessory that'll finish this look off perfectly."

She disappeared back into the store, then returned with a studded leather collar and a long black leash.

"If you wore this with Hannah leading you on a tether, you'd leave zero doubt as to your position in the pecking order."

I paused for a moment, then looked at the two of them with an incredulous expression.

"Are you *kidding* me?" I said. "You think it'll be sexy leading me around like a dog on a *leash*?!"

"Well, you *did* say you wanted to see how far we could take this," Hannah smiled. "This would be pretty much taking it to the maximum degree."

"I've never really been in a lesbian bar before," I said. "What if everybody just wants to paw and molest me when they see me in this thing? Are you going to protect me if things get a little out of control?"

"Of course," Hannah said. "You're still my best friend. I wouldn't let anything happen to you that you didn't feel comfortable doing. But you shouldn't close your mind too much about exploring the possibilities with this scenario. You might actually *enjoy* the kind of attention you're likely to attract from certain members of the lesbian subculture.

"Just how dark does it *get* in these kinds of bars?" I said, peering at the bright overhead lights above me in the dressing room. "I'm going to feel pretty self-conscious if they can see my exposed body as easily as you can in here."

"It's a lot darker than *this*, believe me," Hannah said. "It *is* a pick-up bar, after all. There'll be a lot of extra-curricular activity going on in the corners. Don't worry–you won't be the *only* one attracting the attention of the circling wolves."

"Okay," I said, beginning to relax. "I'm willing to give it a try at least this once. I mean, how bad can it be, right? I'm the one who's ultimately in charge of what happens to my body."

"Exactly," Hannah said, turning her wrist to peer at her watch. "Come on. Let's get you home and lolled up to make you as irresistible as possible. I'm just as excited as you to witness the sexual dynamic in this situation.

After we drove back to Hannah's place, she had me sit down at her make-up table while she fussed over my mascara, eyebrows, and lipstick. After we were all done, we finished off the ensemble with a pair of six-inch-high stilettos, which I thought made me look even *more* like a cheap hooker.

"You're certainly not going to have any trouble attracting every red-blooded lesbian alpha in the room tonight," Hannah said, licking her lips at me. "I'd jump you *myself* right now if you weren't already bound up in that skin-tight costume."

I looked at Hannah with a raised eyebrow and smiled.

"There's still plenty of openings for you to have your way with me. Do you want to have another go with your big purple dildo?"

"Maybe later," Hannah chuckled. "Right now, I'm more excited to see how all the *other* lesbian women react to you. Let's go–it's getting close to prime time."

Hannah and I drove over to the East side where we pulled into a large parking lot next to an industrial building painted in all black. A small neon sign hung over the entrance door flashing *Sappho* in pink letters. I could see a small group of women dressed up in torn jeans and spiky colored hair loitering near the door smoking cigarettes. They looked at our car when we pulled up, then resumed talking amongst themselves.

"Are you sure this is a good idea?" I said, looking at the bare-armed, tattooed girls standing by the door.

"Of course," Hannah said. "It'll be fun. Just lose yourself in the role, and see how it plays out. If you're not digging it, let me know and we can take off whenever you've had enough."

"Okay," I said, wondering what the hell I'd gotten myself into.

Hannah fished around in her purse then pulled out the leather collar and attached it around my neck, snapping on the leather leash and opening her door.

"You sit tight while I come around the other side to get you. If we're going to do this, we might as well play the roles to the full extent for the maximum effect."

"Yes, Master," I said, smiling at her with an obedient expression.

Hannah walked around to the other side of the car, then opened my door and picked up the leash, pulling me gently out of the car. When she led me around the back of the car and the women by the door caught sight of my outfit with Hannah leading me by the leash, everybody stopped talking and stared at me dumbfounded. Hannah simply pretended like everything was normal and walked nonchalantly past the crowd, nodding to a doorman who waved us past the door into the dark and noisy club.

When we entered the main room, there was a female impersonator singing a song on stage with a group of women dancing in the corner. As we headed over to the bar, all the girls milling nearby turned to look at the two of us, running their eyes up and down my body and staring at my exposed skin, which flashed like beacons under the overhead strobe light next to my blacked-out costume in the dark and musky room.

When we finally got to the bar, I tried to position myself in such a way to show the minimum amount of skin, but no matter which way I turned, I was either showing my bare-assed buttocks or exposed breasts and crotch.

"Jesus, Hannah," I said, cozying up to her as close as possible, trying to gain a modicum of cover. "This is even worse than I imagined. My exposed skin looks like its coated with fluorescent *paint* in this place. And everybody is staring at me!"

"I know," she smiled, motioning for the bartender to bring us some drinks. "Isn't it great? Don't you feel sexy dressed up showing off your best assets? If you wanted to play the submissive, this is your chance to test it on the ultimate stage. Just relax and enjoy all the attention. We've got the whole night ahead of us."

When the bartender arrived, Hannah ordered two mai tais and when he placed them on the counter in front of us, I grabbed one of the glasses, taking healthy gulp of the liquid courage.

"Just be cool, girl," Hannah said, pulling gently on my leash while wrapping her hand around the other end resting on the bar. "I got you. I mean, I really *got* you. No one's going to do anything either one of us wants them to do to you as long as they see who owns you."

"Okay," I said, beginning to feel the tension in my body relax as I shifted my weight slightly back from the bar. After a few minutes, a burly girl with a barbell stud in her lower lip approached the two of us, resting a heavily tattooed arm on the bar counter next to me.

"What's up, girl?" she said, glancing down at my protruding tits, pinched even tighter by the constricting black vinyl fabric. "That's quite a hot costume you're wearing."

"Um–thanks," I said, shifting my weight defensively to my other leg closest to Hannah.

"So what's your story?" she said, placing her other hand on my exposed ass while caressing my bare buttocks. "Are you two looking for a little fun, or is this a closed-loop kind of relationship?"

"That depends on what kind of mood my girl is in," Hannah said, eyeing the woman suspiciously while she looked down at her molesting hand disapprovingly. "She's *my* girl, but I might be interested in sharing the spoils if the mood strikes. What do you say, Jade? Do you want to find a private corner and explore some of the boundaries?"

I shifted my weight closer to Hannah while rubbing my body against her, signaling my interest in remaining fully under her control for the time being.

"I'm pretty happy staying with you right now, Master," I said, rubbing my ass against her hip to demonstrate my subordination.

"You heard the girl, *bitch*," Hannah said, swiping the woman's hand away from my ass. "Take your hands off her. This one's *mine*. Go find somebody else to play with."

"Whatever," the girl said, backing away from the bar and uttering a few curse words as she disappeared into the crowd.

"Well, I guess that's *one* way to attract the dominant wolves in the pack," I sighed, turning to take another gulp of my drink.

"You're not feeling the sexual energy so far?" she said, peering around at the other people in the bar.

"Not with *that* one at least," I said. "She was coming on a little too strong. Plus, she wasn't really my type. I don't mind mixing it up with a strong-minded woman, maybe just someone a little hotter, you know?"

"Yeah," Hannah nodded. "I get your drift."

She ordered another round of drinks, then yanked me gently by my harness, leading me across the room to a padded lounge in the corner of the bar where a group of attractive women were chatting amongst themselves and cheering while they watched the performer on the stage. As we approached their table, Hannah motioned with her head to gain their attention momentarily.

"Have you got room for two more?" she said. "We could use a more comfortable spot to sit down, and you girls look like you're up for a little fun."

"Absolutely, one of the women with shorter hair said, pushing the rest of the girls over to make room for us in the middle of the circular seat cushion. "Feel free to get nice and cozy right here between the group of us. It's got the best view of the stage."

Hannah squeezed past the girls on one side of settee, pulling me by the leash as I followed her submissively, taking a spot framed by the first girl and another one with tattooed arms beside me.

"I haven't seen you two in here before," the lead girl sitting next to Hannah said. "Were you just looking to take in the show, or were you looking for a *different* kind of action?"

"We're just kind of playing it as it goes," Hannah said, glancing over at the performer on the stage vamping it up as she sang the Melissa Etheridge anthem Come to my Window. "She's pretty good. She kind of even *looks* a bit like Melissa Etheridge."

"That's the whole idea," the girl said, holding her hands over her crotch like she was grabbing a cock. "But everybody knows she's got some *different* equipment to work with."

"Yeah, I can see that," Hannah said, noticing the singer's Adam's Apple bobbing up and down while she sang.

"Not like your *friend* here," the girl said, staring at my exposed tits poking out above the table. "She's got *all* the right equipment to work with."

Hannah peered over at me silently to see if I was receptive to the obvious advances of the girl, and I smiled at her blankly, taking another swig of my drink. The two alcoholic beverages were already making me a bit tipsy having only eaten a small salad all day, and I slumped back in the chair, resting my head against the padded back-rest. Taking this as a signal of receptivity, the girl sitting next to me raised her glass off the table, rubbing it gently against my exposed nipples. I enjoyed the sensation of the cool surface against my skin, and I slunk further down in my chair, feeling my nipples harden from the combined stimulation of the chilly glass and the rest of the girls watching me from the other side of the table.

"Mmm," the girl next to me hummed, glancing over at Hannah. "I think she likes this. I bet she's a very attentive slave when you need her to be."

"When I *want* her to be," Hannah said, winking at me playfully.

"Oh yeah?" the girl said, reaching her other hand under the table. "What does she like to do? Or should I say, what is she best at *giving*?"

"She's good at *everything*, when she's in the right mood," Hannah smiled. "Am I right, Jade? You kind of *like* it when someone else is in charge, don't you?"

I nodded demurely as I felt the girl's warm hand caressing my bald pussy, running her fingers gently up and down my moistening slit. As her fingers danced over my clit, I couldn't help spreading my legs further apart, getting increasingly turned on by all the attraction around the table. It was kind of fun being the center of attention in our corner of the room, and I could feel my pussy getting wetter and wetter as the rest of the girls' eyes widened while they licked their lips as my seatmate played with my pussy.

After a few minutes of teasing me with her fingers, she grew increasingly bold with her exploration, and when I began to rock my hips in appreciation of what she was doing, she suddenly thrust three fingers deep into my cunt and began ramming her hand hard against my crotch as she leaned over to suck on my nipples into her mouth. I could feel myself getting increasingly turned on by all the stimulation in the public setting, and as I began to moan softly and begin to gyrate in my seat, two of the girls on the other side of the booth ducked underneath the table and crawled toward me, licking and nibbling on the insides of my legs.

They pushed my knees further apart and when their mouths reached my now-dripping pussy, the girl next to me removed her fingers from my hole, allowing the other girls to lick and lap up my juices in a combined two-person assault on my snatch. When the girl beside me began to pinch one of my hardened nipples and flick her fingernail against the flexing teat, the girl sitting next to Hannah couldn't resist any longer and reached over in front of her, rolling my other nipple hard between her fingers. Without any sign of protest on my part, she crawled overtop of Hannah who saw that I was enjoying all the attention, then she straddled my hips facing toward me as she ground her hips into my hard mound.

At first, I enjoyed the combined attention of the swarming mob, but as they grew increasingly rough and bold with their exploration of my body, I began to tense up. While I enjoyed the stimulation from a sexual point of view, I was beginning to feel a bit claustrophobic in the tight confines of the cloistered booth, and I began to pull my thighs together to deter the two women under the table from taking any further liberties.

But instead of reading my signal to back off, they yanked my legs even wider apart while taking turns ramming their fingers into me and lapping up the juices coating the inside of my thighs. When the butchy girl on top of me began kissing down the side of my neck and biting the muscle on top of my shoulder hard enough to cause me pain, I started to push back, trying to signal that I was beginning to feel uncomfortable with how they were taking advantage of me.

But between the action of the girl on top of me pulling me hard against the back of the cushion with her outstretched arms and the girl next to me pinching my nipples tightly and the two girls under the table taking turns ramming their fingers into me up to their knuckles, I was began to panic, and I pushed back more forcefully against the woman pinning me to the cushion while trying to close my thighs against the combined strength of the two women under the table.

When Hannan saw the panic in my eyes and my desperate attempts to free myself from the combined press of the four women, she reached out to the girl sitting on top of me, temporarily pulling her shoulders away from my pinned body.

"I think my girl's had enough of your attention for the time being," she said. "Can't you read the signals? I think she wants you to back off."

"I haven't heard her say stop yet," the girl on top of me said, yanking her body back against my torso with her strong arms, pressing me tightly against the back of the cushion.

"What do you say, Jade?" Hannah said, looking at me to affirm her suspicions. "Have you had enough for now?"

"Yes," I said. "This getting to be a bit too much."

"You heard the girl," Hannah said, trying to pull the big girl's shoulders away from me.

"*Back off*, bitch," she said, swiping Hannah's hand away forcefully. "*You're* the one that brought this slave into our booth. You can have her back when we're finished with her."

"I'm sorry but that doesn't work for me," Hannah said, suddenly grabbing the woman's hair with two hands and yanking her backwards toward the table. "You heard the lady. No means no."

With her nostrils flaring and her eyes filled with rage, she slammed the girl's head hard against the top of the wooden table, momentarily stunning her. Then Hannah stood up on the settee, kicking the woman's head sitting next to me, snapping it backwards. Then she scampered over the top of the table and pulled the woman onto the floor in one swift move, glaring at the rest of the women around the table. Then she grabbed my hand and pulled me off the bench, freeing me from the grasp of the other two women under the table.

"Anyone *else* want to see who's in charge here?" she glared at the rest of the stunned girls sitting around the table. "Come on, baby, let's get the fuck out of this dive. These aren't the kind of chicks that deserve your attention."

Hannah unclipped the leash from my collar and threw it on the floor, then threaded her arm between mine and pushed her way through the club until we spilled out the exit door, breathing in the fresh air from the parking lot.

"I'm sorry, Jade," she said, peering at me as she pushed my ruffled hair to one side. "I didn't know things were going to get that quickly out of control in there."

"Yeah," I said, shaking my head, still in shock. "I think I've had my fill of this whole dom and submissive thing. Although I gotta say, you really turned me on with that whole alpha-wolf, kick-ass performance in there. Where did *that* come from?"

"I just kind of lost control when I saw how they were taking advantage of my best friend and starting to hurt you. I'd never stand by when I saw someone trying to do anything to you that you weren't enjoying."

"Thanks, hun," I said, throwing my arms around her. "Can we go home now and make love the way we used to? You know, when neither one of us is thinking about who's in charge or who's on the top or the bottom. I just want to make love like we're *equals* again."

"Absolutely," Hannah said. "I think I learned just as much from this little experiment as you. Ultimately, every successful relationship depends on mutual respect and consent. It's fine to play master and submissive every now and then, but only with the underpinnings of a real abiding love. Otherwise, it can quickly devolve into an unhealthy dynamic."

"I couldn't have said it better myself," I said, kissing her gently on the cheek. "Come on, there's someone *else* I feel like sharing the love with right now..."

W*ant more all-girl erotic chills and thrills? Download the next volume in the discounted collection:*

No boys allowed...

Sneak peek:

When the rest of the girls began to realize what the three of us were up to, it didn't take long for the entire group to devolve into a moaning, slithering mass of naked bodies writhing under the thick jumble of cotton robes and woolen blankets. I pulled Fatima's dress all the way over her shoulders and squeezed her bare tits while she played with my clit and moaned into my mouth...

READ MORE

MORE FROM VICTORIA RUSH:

Choose your next toe-curling fantasy from over thirty-five spicy stories in Jade's Erotic Adventures. Browse the full collection here:

Click to scan your favorites...

FOLLOW VICTORIA RUSH:

Want to keep informed of my latest erotic book releases? Sign up for my newsletter and receive a FREE bonus book:

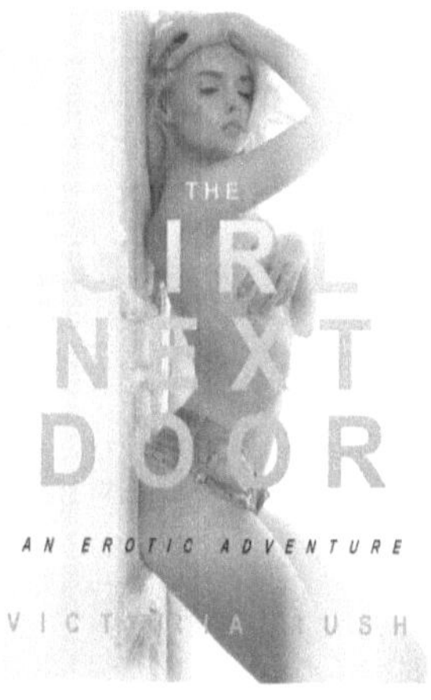

Spying on the neighbors just got a lot more interesting...